Juliette T. Burton

The Five Jewels of the Orient

Juliette T. Burton

The Five Jewels of the Orient

ISBN/EAN: 9783337331825

Printed in Europe, USA, Canada, Australia, Japan

Cover: Foto ©Andreas Hilbeck / pixelio.de

More available books at **www.hansebooks.com**

THE

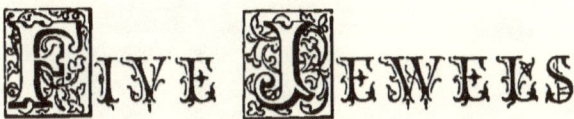

FIVE JEWELS

OF THE

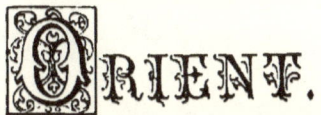

ORIENT.

BY

JULIETTE T. BURTON.

NEW YORK:
MASONIC PUBLISHING COMPANY,
626 BROADWAY.
1872.

DEDICATION.

I AFFECTIONATELY DEDICATE THIS BOOK

TO THE

SISTERS OF THE EASTERN STAR,

TRUSTING THAT EACH ONE MAY FIND

PROFITABLE RECREATION

FROM A PERUSAL OF ITS PAGES.

Preface.

RUE merit speaks for itself; it is useless to eulogize that which does not really bear intrinsic worth, for whatever is flimsy, trashy, or unstable, will, of itself, fall to pieces, despite all the praise that may be heaped around.

When one writes, if there is originality, it will at once strike the critical reader; if there is a reasonable basis, it will be seen; and if things are said which stir the fountains of feeling, they will be appreciated to their full value.

We agree that when a woman writer puts *finis* to manuscript, and gives it over to her publisher, she experiences somewhat the feelings of a mother whose daughter has just been married; *she* believes in the virtues of her child, but is fearful that another may not perceive them, and not until after the first issue does she feel certain that the shoals of disappointment are safely passed.

We shall, in some of the succeeding sketches, take up the general routes which have been well trod by previous writers, shall borrow the same strain that has been sung, but perhaps by some peculiarity of style, and through different authority than has been heretofore referred to, we may be able to stop at villas, to drink of fountains, traverse romantic paths that others had not discovered, and in our relations present other curious features to our readers.

Plain matter-of-fact relations of incident in biographies seldom please; romance *must* gild a tale to make it agreeable. Without romance all creations would be dull; man would be a barbarian, woman a nonentity; wisdom, genius, liberty, would be indifferently regarded, and the very heavens, even, would seem dim.

It was under a romantic guise that Christ was born and walked the earth; he taught by parables, and mellow prose poems were his familiar speech; his life and martyrdom were typified by symbols, and even the advent of the Spirit in form of a dove was more novel and attractive than any usual mode of communicating would have been. Mythology, the exquisiteness of romance, by its peculiar presentation of truth and virtue, founded the divine institution of Freemasonry. The whole stream of sentient existence has its spring-time of romance, and old age does not forget it.

High coloring cannot *create* merit, but *may surround* it, and attract attention to modest worth which might otherwise never be brought forward to the observation of the best. We hope that the true lustre of our Five Jewels may shine into the hearts of all who love virtue, and that the Sisters of the Eastern Star *especially* may find traits of excellence, worthily depicted, in their histories.

Prelude.

Ah! this earth would be cold if the blush of romance
    Was chased from its surface entire,
If the pulse of man's mind could no longer enhance
    The tone of life's every-day lyre.

If the ideal veil should be suddenly lift,
    To leave the nude object bereft
Of the numerous graces of drapery's gift,
    But half of its beauty'd be left.

Should the magical stream of romance never lave,
    The root of the cherished "Roof-Tree,"
There would never hang garlands of fame for the brave,
    And the "mistletoe bough" wouldn't be.

1*

Should woman divorce from her pathway this ray,
    Where the roses are—might come the thorn;
And the blisses that *now* into man's bosom pay,
    Might have in their stead—hope forlorn.

'Tis the sorcerer's wand that most cunningly gilds
    Existence's rough places o'er;
The prose-ground enchanted, where poesy builds
    Its love-lighted halls evermore.

'Tis the panacea mixed with stern duty's demand
    That sweetens the gall in each cup;
And chained to the clod would our hopes ever stand,
    If its light wing ne'er lifted them up.

When Youth from Life's volume by Time has been chased,
    And senility opens its page,
'Tis the pencil by which every record is traced
    That brings joy to the eye of old age.

                          JULIETTE T. BURTON.

Contents.

Illustrations.

Ode to the Eastern Star.

When the scene of life changes from pleasure to gloom,
And the soul sees its midnight uncheered by a ray ;
When the spirit droops low 'neath the weight of its doom,
As the hopes that once lighted its halls die away ;
Then there shines through the windows of heaven afar
Bright gleams that bring peace from a beautiful Star,
The Star of the East, that most beautiful Star.

When the willows are waving o'er graves wherein lie
The first-born of mothers, whose tears will not dry ;
Or the widow bends crushed with the blight of despair,
All the comfort departed that made life so fair ;
Then there comes through the vista of sorrow afar,
For the cheerless a light from a beautiful Star,
The Star of the East, that most beautiful Star.

May harmony bring in its circle of light
All the colors that make up a halo as bright
As charity, patience, long-suffering, and love,
Can catch from reflection of Jewels above,
Which shine through celestial gates set ajar ;
In blessing and peace on our beautiful Star.

Juliette T. Burton.

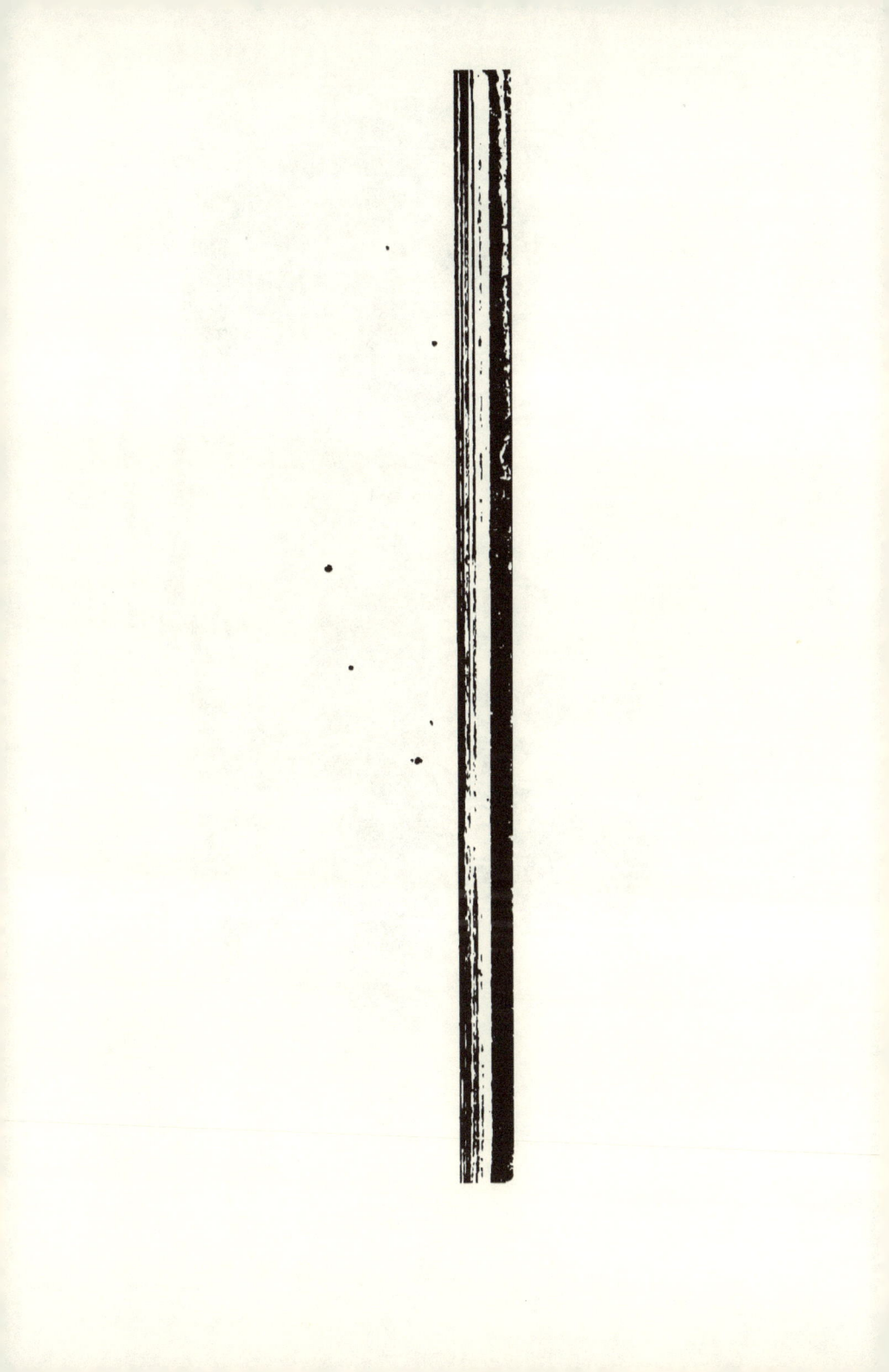

THE TURQUOISE BEFORE JEPHTHAH.

I.

The Turquoise.

ADAH.

"She was his only child; besides her he had neither son nor daughter."

THESE words at once suggest a volume of possibilities, unfold a sacred page, indite a tender strain, and draw a holy picture. Man's nature, corrugated to suit his sphere of practical contact with discordant or opposing elements, has, reserved, beneath those hard rinds, a sweet sap of sentiment for the tenderer handling of woman; a secret, interior, accordant instrument of the soul, his heart of hearts, which but a few, in any man's lifetime, may play upon.

There are mere surfaces of feeling which graduate
from the positively stern, and *these* may be caught
by occasional passions and mellowed for the moment, but, like tracks in the sand, they pass away.
Not so with this inner music; its strains, once
awoke, can never cease vibration, and will be sacred
to one master-hand alone. That master-hand may
not always know its capabilities to torture or to
soothe. Happy, thrice happy, the man who has for
his genius one who will not awaken weird, wild
notes of distortion, but who will woo the tenderest
pathos of enjoyment.

Jephthah, the hunter, the judge, the mighty man
of valor, before whom none stood in point of execu-
tive force of will, whose brawny figure might be
likened to the mountain-side—for his thews and
sinews stood out like roots; his grizzly beard tossed
about by his motions looked like vines swayed by
the wind; his eyes were brilliant as the sun's rays
reflected from granite; and his voice was loud like
the roar of the cataract—Jephthah, the iron man,
had yet, beneath all this exterior hardness, the clear
running fountain of paternal love, which could be

played in every variation of delight by the magic touch of his only child—a daughter.

Of all states of perfection to which a woman may aspire, none is more divine than that of filial devotion. In the truly amiable *daughter* may be found the germs of all other fitness; sister, wife, and mother are born out of a good daughter, and man need never fear to choose for *wife* the woman who has nobly sustained that relation. In the Bible history, singularly enough, there is no personal appellative signified to the heroine of so much tragical romance. She is called throughout simply "Jephthah's daughter." Modern associations attach to their symbolical representations of this character the name of Adah, whose poetical definition is "powerful perfume, or strength and sweetness," and we will occasionally, for the sake of clearness, call Jephthah's daughter, Adah.

She was of the fairness of the moon, the brightness of the stars, and the goodness of the summer dews, to use oriental descriptiveness; in less equivocal terms, we might draw her picture, and for a perfect portrait refer all to Doré's most exquisite

painting of " Jephthah's daughter and the maidens,
on the mountain bewailing her sad fate." No houri
of Arabic celebrity, or peri of oriental verse, was
ever more beautiful in form and feature: the lus-
ciousness of perfect proportion, with the rich tints
of high color, made her surpassingly attractive in
mere *physique*, while the *soul*, that was fitted to the
very highest tone of moral and virtuous principle,
reflected through her countenance its marvellous
finish, glorifying the *flesh* into a spiritual loveliness. Her mind was cultivated; for from all of
the barbaric or heathenish ages there have been
handed down to us records of the educational rules
of the period; and whether or not it lay in the same
line of orthography with modern schools, it was sufficient to enlighten the pupil up to its own period.

She was a skillful housewife. From her infancy
she had had no mother, and had stood at the head
of her father's household. The women of that day
were skilled in knitting, weaving, and embroidering
dexterously, the most cunning articles of exquisite
design and finish; and although the most patrician
dame, as well as the plebeian maid, took part in

servile work when the occasion became imperative,
yet the hands of Adah showed no signs of rough
occupation; they were fair and stainless, and were
well adapted to silk embroidery. Women dyed
beautiful colors; and some of the most enterprising
were engaged in trade,—dealt in purple dye-stuffs
alone. These dyes were to be had, after much peril
and cost, from foreign lands. Woman was a trader,
and engaged in ordinary merchandise then, as well
as now, as in the book of Proverbs may be found
the words: "She maketh fine linen, and selleth it,
and delivereth it to her merchant." Before the time
that Adah became old enough to realize the need
of a mother's tender training, she was deprived of
that mother, and afterward was grieved sorely and
painfully at the oft-repeated absences of her father
from home.

Many and painful were the periods of separation
from her sole guardian and friend, for his habits as
hunter, and afterward as general of a great army,
subjected him to innumerable perils, of which the
quick perception and keen affection of Adah always
apprized her. His love was to her all that made

the skies seem bright; an assurance of his personal
safety was essential to her happiness. Often, when
in company with men of roving habits, wild rangers
of the borders, spoilers and banditti, he would call
for his black steed; which, like his master, "scented
the battle afar," and was anxious to be gone. Adah
would on those occasions fasten his war-harness
around him : her delicate hands buckled the armor,
while her white teeth gleamed from between lips
which parted in smiles, yet which only smiled to
hide the tears that were crowding to her eyes, yet
these, as a soldier's daughter, she heroically commanded to stay. She longed for the days of warfare
and violence to cease, and prayed from a heart of
piety—emotive prayer. Constitutional, spontaneous
devotion was her habit. Prayer not left to grow
stagnant, and only to burst out on some great occasion into jets of sensibility, but which arose with
the morning sun, and only ceased when sleep settled
upon her. To pray was to her a necessity : to
whom could she tell the terrible anxieties which her
filial affection, in the exigencies of her father's
peculiar life, induced ? To the Lord God of Israel,

JEPHTHAH AND HIS COMPANIONS RETURNING FROM A MARAUDING EXPEDITION.

she looked for consolation; from Him alone might
any comfort come. Many a time Adah gazed up
at the stars which shine so directly down from the
cloudless azure-tinted heavens of the Orient, and
tried, by invocation, to penetrate the veil that cur-
tained between her and the Divinity. Devout joy
was native to her temperament, and was heightened by the sweet entertainment she gave it. ·By
giving the history, cursorily, of Jephthah, we may
with more facility glide into the drama of Adah's
subsequent story.

Jephthah, it is stated, was an illegitimate son of
Gilead, whose wife had other sons. These sons were
enraged and jealous at Jephthah's sharing with them
their patrimonial rights; and when they grew up
they forcibly expelled him from their premises.

In his exile, being too proud to dig, or beg,
he conceived a taste for the sword, and joined
to himself men of lascivious habits, extravagant,
reckless, who by their own extravagance were
reduced to poverty; and with such he marauded
the borders. By his intrepidity, and wonderful
prowess in arms, Jephthah soon gained high

renown for bravery, strategy, and success; and when Israel was very sorely distressed by the Ammonites, and when they found themselves incompetent to organize their numbers into military order, and they could not find among them a leader, the elders assembled and unanimously declared Jephthah the nominee for general-in-chief of their armies. It seems that this was a sore reflection upon the children of Israel, and proves that it must have been through disobedience and alienation from the laws of their religion, that they were now reduced to such a necessity as that of calling upon one who was by Jewish law not fit for the place; for, " He who was the son of a harlot might in no wise rule among them."

But necessity overcomes many scruples, and the elders themselves made most flattering concessions to Jephthah, hoping to gain his consent; and they said to him, " Come, and be our captain." They tried to flatter him with allusions to his martial genius, their conviction of his bravery, and used every inducement to influence him to become their leader. Jephthah would not at first be prevailed upon to accept command of the army, urging as objection that some of his brothers who had persecuted him were among the elders. So far is the prejudice of man sometimes carried, that no prospect of personal aggrandizement is sufficient to wipe off wrongs, or to reconcile them to close contact with those toward whom they have once formed strong dislikes. It is a strict rule in *Israelitish law to defend the poor and fatherless*; this his brothers had failed to do in his own case ; he wished them to realize their own injustice before he could consent to become a leader for his country. His patriotism was zealous, but his prejudice was stronger; and not until after *much* persuasion, and their consenting to conform to his prescribed terms, would he be prevailed upon to become their chief. We cannot admire the general tenor of Jephthah's early life, yet must give him praise for an independence of mind, a heroic fortitude, which could .alone have induced him to decline again, even after his brothers had made concession, a place that he felt was one of such honor, that only the positive necessity of the moment could have instigated them to offer it to him.

2

Jephthah said unto the elders of Gilead : "Did you not hate me, and expel me out of my father's house ? and why are ye come unto me now in distress ?" And the elders among whom were his brothers, entreated him to come, described the unfortunate condition of the Jews who had gone astray after idols, and pointed to the probability of their deliverance, not only from their enemies, but from further wickedness, if he would agree to become their leader. So at last, Jephthah, unable to withstand their repentance, after he had stipulated with them for certain conditions, consented to be their captain. He required them to sign a pledge to this effect : If he returned successful from his battles, they would still retain him for their leader. This they did.

Jephthah had learned in his experience of shifts, amidst every variety of mind, that a man may be exalted when expediency renders it necessary for the general good, but that when events settle down ordinarily, the same man is apt to be let sink back into his original obscurity ; as the necessity for his effort is removed he becomes useless as an ornament, and is consequently forgotten.

Jephthah had some ambition; and a strong incentive worked the lever of his aspirations. He remembered the fresh rose that bloomed in his bower, and liked to shed lustre over it, through valorous deeds and well-earned praise. His heart also repented it, of the lawless habits which he had assumed; and he determined to reform his hitherto wild, reckless life, and to become a man honored among men, and approved by the God of his forefathers, from whom he had strayed.

No one who seriously reflects upon the disadvantage under which he labored when a child—for from his very birth he had lived among boys who were selfish, avaricious, and entirely ignorant of the principles of the beautiful laws of Jewish equity, which handled each man, woman, and child, under every circumstance and condition, as tenderly as justice would allow, boys who scrupled not to heap insult upon injury, who taunted him with the sins of his mother, derided with jeers and laughter every sign of chivalric conduct, and set at naught his youthful exploits—nobody could wonder at his irregular habits after he became a man. And again *he had no mother*

_____

to watch over him, and this is a whole argument against probable morality in any man.

He was a child born neither of a wife, a concubine, nor a mistress, but of a stray woman, whose position excluded the son from recognition in any plane of social obligation : he was taken into the house of his father's wife, who jealously and hatefully regarded him as the usurper of her lawfully-born children's rights, and she urged her rude sons by her example to their course of cruelty toward the orphan.

To crush down an independent, high spirit, by sneers, to keep ambition tied hand and foot by pecuniary poverty, is like fastening a lion, fresh from the wild woods, the broad forests, rolling tides of waters, the clear, free, unfettered light of heaven, the liberty that Nature gives, in a cage half-dark ; and leads to perverted talent, vitiated tastes, and corrupt habits.

Cruelty to his manliness, hatred of his name, and contempt for his society, were hard things for a proud lad to bear; and when his brothers, determined that he should no longer live with them, and by brute force overcame the father's authority and Jephthah's strength, and thrust him forth into the

wide world, alone, without a resting-place for his
head besides the ground, or a roof to shelter him besides the canopy of the skies, without woman's hand
to smooth a single hardship from his path, and with
scarcely any conception of God's love for each one of
his chosen race ; it is not strange that Jephthah in
his undisciplined state of mind should cultivate the
fiercer passions, and for expression of them, take
delight in daring exploits, startling adventures, and
dangerous feats.

Jephthah's life, from the time that he was a youth
of perhaps eighteen to full manhood, was not filled
with commissions of willful sin, but his lawlessness
was rather the result of biased circumstances. Such
a life is not so heinous in the eye of Omnipotence,
as the transgressions of moral law which men of cultivated minds and golden opportunity often weave
over great spaces of their lives, transgressions upon
which the eye of respectability has not rested and
named *crime;* sins which have been wrapped up
under the extenuating circumstance of wealth, or
hidden behind the sanctity of ecclesiastical dignity ;
yet which, for all that, are in reality, deepening

and tightening their folds, hardening, all the time, the fibres of moral being. When at the bar of immortal judgment these men stand together, Jephthah may be the first to reach forth and take the sceptre of love, and the sign of retribution.

Circumstance is the grand shaper of human conduct; principle is often subordinate to its stern relations. Fact is fact; and necessity is invincible.

It is not stated in Sacred history, nor in any commentary, where Jephthah married his wife, but when he left his native place he went to Tob, whose poetic interpretation is "good, pleasant, agreeable;" and as he became associated with men, some of whom had held high places, were rich and influential at one time, it is probable that in one of these families he found an accomplished, lovely woman, who, under the inspiration of love, forgetting or not knowing the discrepancies in their social spheres, married him. Jephthah became rich through his spoils, and was afterward renowned for his mighty deeds in arms; possibly grief at the daily-increasing jeopardy in which the life of her idolized husband was placed induced premature disease and conse-

quently the wife's death, when Adah was at a very
tender age.

It was the custom in ancient days, as well as now,
for ladies of distinction to have numerous servants, a
maid or man-servant to fill every place in the detail
of household economy.   Jephthah's wife was not
without her share of luxury and the usual appointments of ladies of rank.   It was a romantic country,
and was a fit field for cultivating the sentimental or
emotional, and we may fancy Jephthah's bride often
wandering with her maids along flowery foot-paths,
or up steep ravines, and over flimsy foot-bridges,
scanning precipitous heights, where vines of luxuriant fruitage lined the banks around and reached
the topmost boughs of the trees, while the variegated
tints of the plumage of sweet singing-birds made
elegant contrast, and their trills vocalized the air.
Often would she wend her footsteps down the glen,
and across the moor, stretching her gaze afar in
hope of being rewarded by the sight of her lord,
her chief, her hero, her husband, after he had remained absent a longer time than he proposed; and
we can see how the stalwart form of Jephthah tow-

ered above her dimensions, as he, after springing from his foaming steed, and giving a quick glance back at his comrades in the distance, whom he had outridden, opened his arms and fondly embraced his gentle wife, calling her, "his rose," and repaying her, in that one loving caress, for all the tears she had shed on account of his absence.

Some of the most love-sick heroes of romance have been described in Bible history, and the sturdy warriors of that day and time open a wider field for romantic speculation than anything of modern era. All that could be procured to adorn his house for his wife's pleasure, Jephthah secured; no time or expense was spared, whereby her comfort might be established or her pleasures enhanced. Jephthah loved her still more dearly because she had taken him when life had so drear an aspect, and there was nothing in his circumstances which could have presented an inducement for any woman to wish to share. She had made choice of him because of the glory that love, which is so peculiar, so mysterious, had painted about him.

Love, oh! so good, the comforter,
Divinity and arbiter,
Of each one's life; a thing so sweet
It will all difficulties meet.
If it may but *give itself;* It cares
Not for reproach, or blame; but dares.

They loved one another enthusiastically, and when their first-born, their only-born, was given them, their loves were monumented in the sweet little scion of their blent selves.

Desolate and drear, after this dear wife died and was buried in the tombs among her ancestors, would his life have been, if the black-haired babe had not represented her, and as the child grew into womanhood, if she had not been all with which *such* a mother might have endowed her daughter. She inherited every beautiful trait from both parents. She resembled her mother in form and feature. She had imbibed, from the peculiar nature of her father's pursuits, a stronger spirit of endurance, and a keener sense of the duties incumbent upon a soldier's daughter, than her mother, who had been brought up amid the peaceful domestic scenes of

2*

civil life, could ever gain. She was flaccid even,
to the most acute sensibility, yet in moments of
imminent anxiety or impending peril, she could call
up the stern adamantine of self-control to a degree
which some, who called themselves philosophers,
might have been proud to emulate.

In her childhood her father's retainers were wont
to show her the most chivalrous attention, which
early gave an individual strength to her manner, and
created a self-reliance which served a good purpose
in her life of double duty. Adah had a luxuriance
of black hair which waved in rich masses around a
head beautifully shaped. She was remarkable for
the length and texture of her hair, among the
companions with whom she associated. There
were many maidens in Tob, and as her father's
house was well appointed, and an accession of numbers made no material difference in her domestic
arrangement, she had always staying with her five
or six young friends who cheered her in her father's
absence. Many a sweet story of love and valor and
knightly escort would one relate to the others, each
taking their turn to recite. Flowers grew luxuri-

antly in that region. Around her, on every side, Adah was accustomed to glorious colors, sweet scents, and in varieties of rose, lily, and pomegranate. Fresh fountains of water, sending out perpetually their jets like liquid diamonds, shone between the green vesture of the olive and the scarlet of the azalia, making a sylvan-like scene. All these attractions attached this child of beauty to her home, and through the beautiful she was attached to life. Life is desirable; there is enough on this shore to make it enjoyable wherever there is a spirit wise enough to look beyond petty events to the universal grand scheme of eternal good which is in our very midst.

Sweetly sang Adah; tenderly she touched her timbrel; and sometimes her festivals were marked by rare displays of the poetry of motion which terpsichorean amateurs might well praise. Jephthah's daughter was religiously trained; her mother had not been an idolater, but was one of the chosen people; her religious devotions had never been biased by any association with

heathens. Adah also served the God of her fathers
with all the fervor of her ardent nature.

One day, when Adah was seventeen, and the full
beauties of ripeness which had entered into compact to create a faultless living thing were satisfied
that they had clothed her with so celestial a dower
that she stood more like a spiritual vision of angelic
design than as mere woman, she took hold of the
hand of Beta, her favorite companion, and went
toward the foot of a high hill or mountain in the
rear of her house. Not being afraid, they wandered
beyond their destination, and came unexpectedly
upon a band of strange men and women, who were
not called gypsies in those days, but who were verily
of the same kind. They were a mixture of races
for whom we have scarcely a name; offshoots from
tribes who were ostracised from the privileges of
name and nationality; roving and unsettled, but
peaceful. They pitched their tents anywhere, sometimes planting a little colony in a night, making a
lively foreground to the blunt, scraggy mountain-
sides, remaining for a short time, and leaving as
suddenly.

As Adah and her friend wandered out of their
usual route, they came suddenly upon one of these
little encampments of snow-white tents, and turned
to retrace their steps, but a form rose up before Adah, strongly marked against the sky, and
stood as if spell-bound, gazing upon her beauty, of
which, in her innocence of vanity, she did not
think.

It was the form of a man, athletic and symmetri-
cally proportioned; he was graceful, and seemed to
be well versed in the etiquette of the day, for he
took off one of his sandals and laid it upon his head.
This meant, in polite interpretation, humility or
acknowledgment of superiority, either of beauty,
sex, rank, or power. Greatly surprised as she was,
Adah was too kind not to return the salutation, and
when he made known to her that he was her
mother's near relation, and had lately come from
Moab on a visit to Tob, she invited him to come to
her father's house, for the maidens of that time were
hospitable, and it is well remembered to what extent
Rebecca carried this fine quality, in giving, not only
to the messenger at the well water from her pitcher,

but by also watering his camels with her own fair
hands.

Andra was curiously observing the manners of
these people who occupied the tents when the unexpected apparition of his cousin was presented. He
went home with Adah and Beta, where he tarried
until Jephthah returned, by whom he was well received. The modest and dignified customs of the
East, dictated retirement to the females of a house,
not from inferiority of position or servitude of sta-
tion, but because inclination approved of what
custom dictated; but neither was it a sign of rank
to be cold and restrained by artificial laws. Adah,
as mistress of the house, gave kind attention to her
cousin Andra, and sat with him and her father,
manifesting in a hundred ways to the delighted
senses of Andra her superiority and virtue. The
word virtue has its definition in more than one
sense, it implies mental and moral strength, energy,
and resolution.

The sweet-lipped god could not stay away, could
not abide in the distance when there was such delightful opportunity offered for his manifestation,

and before the veiled heart of Adah was fairly alive
to its own susceptibility it was seized, appropriated,
and enlisted under a new order; something so
sweet, so blissful came into her soul in return, that
its excess created a suffusion of blushes upon her
face, a soft languor in her eyes, and a hesitation in
her manner, which declared to Andra that his own
disease was caught, and that each had the other's
symptoms. Such joys as her mother had experienced in the days of her courtship, and as all
women from Eve successively down have realized,
and must still entertain as long as time lasts,
had now sprung up in the fresh soil of her nature
to impress it indelibly. The great inspiration of
this new intelligence is wonderful in forming the
character of a young girl.

Adah had always, from a mere child, assiduously
performed work in the household, and she manifested a judgment and discrimination beyond her
years. Her own fingers worked the elegant curtains
which hung at the oriental doorways, or embroidered the quilted coverlets for the divans. Her ingenuity devised models for vases and frames, with

which her beautiful garden was decorated. The situation and arrangement of the sweet shrubs and flowers were suggested by her, and her own dress was superintended and sometimes partially made by herself. She had naturally a love for gorgeous color; it was what her eye had rested upon from her birth; the amethyst sky at sunset, the mountains tinged with hues of rose, and violet, and orange were familiar to her eye; birds also, varying in tint from every shade of purple to faintest azure, she had always seen. When Andra first met her, she wore an embroidered dress of scarlet with a blue bodice, a thin, white, soft veil which floated around her figure and shaded, without concealing, her features. She was tasteful, industrious, economical, and charitable. She wholly fulfilled the text, "She stretcheth out her hand to the poor; yea, she reacheth forth her hands to the needy." Her charity widened, increased, and encompassed all within her reach. She had been patient under great suspense, and from her religious nature, many doubts must naturally have agitated her mind as to the moral character of her father's life, and her con-

viction of his lack of piety must have pained her.
Young as Adah was, she had had occasion to be
made thoughtful and prudent; she had learned the
true submission of a meek spirit under the dispensa-
tions of life; she had needed but the touch of *love* to
baptize her into *perfect* womanhood; through this
sacrament she now came, and was ready for sacrifice,
or any oblation that circumstance might dictate.

Their union was approved by Jephthah, and the
happy young lover was ready to perform his vows
unto the Lord. Soon after this, Jephthah was so-
licited earnestly to take the lead of the army to
rescue the Israelites from the invasion of the Ammonites and others, to which proposition he finally
assented upon their acceptance of his terms, which
were that he should be made constant Judge of
Israel on his successful return. Though full of
martial impulse, Jephthah was humane, and always
avoided bloodshed if possible; therefore he sent to
the leaders in Ammon terms of capitulation, to
which they returned answer: " That the land of the
Israelites was theirs; that it had originally belonged
to them, from whom it had been taken by the

Amorites, who had been dispossessed by the Israelites; and that on these grounds they claimed the
restitution of their lands."

Jephthah, believing that the land belonged to the
Israelites by right of conquest from the actual possessors, would not recognize any claim of antece-
dent possessors, who not only had rendered them
no help but had showed them some hostility. The
Ammonites reasserted their claims, and on this issue
hostilities were inaugurated.

Before engaging in battle Jephthah vowed a vow
unto the Lord, to be fulfilled in the result of victory. This brings our narrative to the thrilling
and tragical incidents connected with Jephthah's
daughter. The vow which Jephthah so thought-
lessly made was as follows:

" And Jephthah vowed a vow unto the Lord, and
said, If thou shalt without fail deliver the children
of Ammon into my hands, then it shall be that
whatsoever cometh of the doors of my house to
meet me, when I return in peace from the children
of Ammon, shall surely be the Lord's, and I will
offer it up for a burnt-offering."

The general nature of a vow is that of a promissory oath, of future service. Vows were very common under the Old Testament dispensation. Those in distress, sickness, or difficulty, made promises to God of certain stipulated services in the event of their deliverance or success. David says, "Thy vows are upon me, O Lord; I will render praise unto thee, for thou hast delivered my soul from death. Wilt thou not deliver my feet from falling, that I may walk before God in the land of the living?"

Adah, although gentle in disposition, was not without fervid patriotism, and this the recollection of the annals of her kindred and country helped to intensify.

Every sympathetic feeling in her nature was aroused when her father was called to a high post of honor by the elders and rulers, and filial affection, piety, and emotions of ambition for the success of the Israelites stirred her sensibilities. Her interest was doubled in the coming contest when Jephthah selected Andra as one of his officers, *his* fame also becoming involved.

Warfare has, incidental to it, tragedies of fearful
importance. Ancient tradition and modern account
agree that upon its track there follow a succession
of horrible occurrences : the black-winged messenger
of disease, disaster, crime, demoralization ; and that
tragedy becomes habitualized to the hour.

The preparation for a severe conflict at arms
throws a country into a fermentation of excitement ;
martial spirit runs high, ambition forgets the possibility of defeat, and excited imagination crowns every
one a victor. Money flows ; the national exchequer
runs out freely, extravagance knows no stop ; and
men, like puppets, play upon springs which may
snap in a moment, and leave them limp and disabled.

Though anxiety for her father's and lover's safety
greatly agitated Adah's mind, yet she seized the
contagion of hope, and was thrown into the general
feeling which commonly exercised all ; so that she
did not, until the very moment of parting came,
realize the terrible peril in which all who were
dearest to her would be placed.

When the great army, as far as her eye could
reach, was stretched across the plain, awaiting but

the signal of their captain to start for glorious conquest or for sad defeat, Adah, for one moment
forgetful of all save the womanly tenderness in her
heart, twined her arms around Jephthah and pa-
thetically entreated him not to expose, carelessly,
his beloved form to the mark of the enemy. Jephthah held this treasure, prized higher than all earthly things save his honor, to his heart, then placing
her hand in Andra's, turned to his war-horse,
mounted, and was gone.

The maiden raised her face to her lover's, and in
one long, silent kiss, the blisses of love were poured
out, which neither the circumstance of its occasion
nor the possibility of its being final could make less
sweet.   One pressure against his strong breast,
whose emotions were strenuous for love and sacrificial to duty, and he, too, was gone.

Desolate days and nights were passed; through
which Adah shivered under the cruel chill of apprehension. The excitement of preparation being over,
the endurance of separation seemed hard.   The
flowers bloomed as gayly, the birds sang as merrily,
the sky shone as bright, friends surrounded her,

God was above, yet there was a yearning after the
absent ones; a longing for their safety which created
a gloomy mental mist; melancholy settled upon her.
Music could no longer amuse, books no longer
solace, and her handmaidens often found her weep-
ing. It was not for herself that she would have
indulged such sorrow, but for those whose lives,
precious to themselves as well as her, were in peril.

In the meantime Jephthah, girded with his unerr-
ing sword, led his army from the declivities across
Jordan, where the opposing hordes were gathered
as thick as blades of grass. He became inspired
with strength from invisible heavenly powers; the
mantle of valor settled over him; his hands were
controlled and his voice sent commands which were
like utterances of the gods; he dashed upon the
enemy like a falling bolt, amid gleaming spears and
willing blades, and came out clear of wounds, un-
hurt by anything, after hosts had closed again and
again about him. At last, like waves held by the
tide, his enemies fell back; the rout was complete,
Jephthah was victor.

His military tactics proved that no mean master-hand guided him. His religious nature came forth from the obscurity of perverted life, his vow returned to him after the success of his arms; and he praised God in his heart, and determined by the pious observance of that vow to expiate some of his past offences against divine law.

He sent a herald before him to apprize his beloved only child, who could touch the springs of his nature as none other might, of his victory and immediate return.

Joy, unqualified delight, flooded Adah's heart. Her country was saved; her father and lover left alive; were both made famous by their intrepidity and superior generalship! Smiles wreathed her face, all of the sleeping animation was restored, and the very goddess of pleasure herself might have patterned expressions from Adah's eyes, lips, and whole countenance.

Rejoicing was the motive of the hour; families and people all with one heart, acclamatory of praise, lifted their voices in thanksgiving. Only those who have lived in the midst of war can realize how gratefully *peace* comes.

Jephthah's daughter had cause to make great demonstration, and she called together hastily her household, and arranged with them plans for a festival. Rich cakes, preserves, and confectionery, meats and strong food, wine, nectarines, and grapes, were all gathered, arranged, and set in the grand hall for the returning generals and soldiers. Great was the excitement of the servants and maidens. Adah went around like a white, misty cloud, dropped a word here and there, or peeped over some gardener's brawny shoulder, with a smile which outshone the summer light that ravished his flowers, and repaid him for the wounds of thorns (which, alas! will grow everywhere), or the wanton riot set loose among his favorite beds and borders.

Beauty sits well in every place; it can never be disproportioned to circumstance, but, like the sunlight, can measure any distance or fill any space. And Adah, under the shadow of the peasant's lintel, or within the brilliant light of palace-hall, was still a welcome object. And now, in this hour of triumph, many who had been blessed by her hand came and brought offerings of sweet laurels or some

tender token of their appreciation, and Adah gladly
received every kind demonstration. At last, after
everything necessary for her feast had been prepared, the table spread, festoons of flowers hung in a
triumphal arch in front of her doorway, the maidens
assembled, she awaited the approach of her father
and her lover.

She had thought that, to please her lover, she
would put on bridal attire, and it is possible that
sweet visions of her nuptials actuated her. White
embroidered silk, with a tunic over it of soft, float-
ing, silver tissue, composed her dress. Pearls were
around her wrists and arms above the elbows;
around her neck, in her ears were large hoops of
gold set with pearls. A white veil floated over her
flowing hair, and gave to it the appearance of frost
upon a raven's wing. We can imagine her eager-
ness for the meeting, how breathlessly she awaited
the first intimation of their approach.

> With their harps and timbrels strung,
> Upon expectancy they hung;
> As, bending o'er, each lovely maid
> Her tribute of attention paid.

3

The welcome signal came at last;
One sigh from parted lips she cast;
Then Adah floated forth to treat
The heroes, with her greeting sweet.

Like visions caught in happy dream
The scene presented here might seem,
'Twas if as angels, bright, had dropt
From paradise, and warfare stopt.

For grizzled warriors, whose arms
Were tremulous of late alarms,
And glittering steel, whose ardent track
Was scored in blood, gave back.

They made betwixt a pathway that
The maid might reach him, who still sat
Upon his steed, whose long locks caught
By whipping winds to curls were wrought.

His beard uncombed, in battle trim,
Was knotted on his breast; and grim
The warrior seemed, although
His eye burned with a tender glow.

Beneath the rugged outside stirred
A thought of sweets to fame preferred;
His "singing-bird" invoked the strain,
And Adah ruled the chief again.

Visions of her glad face and thoughts of the happy meeting indeed played through his brain and heart, and his aspiration took a high tone; he praised God for his victories, for the gift of his child, and determined to live in the future as became a judge in Israel, and the father of *such* a daughter. Just as his spirit seemed sweetened to its very tenderest tone, he observed the swaying of his guard; and lo! through the avenue came flying a white cloud. God of Israel! 'twas his child, his Adah, his singing-bird, his lamb, his ring-dove, his bond to earth, his inspiration for heaven. She; she was to be offered up a living human sacrifice.

Mechanically, in obedience to her loved voice, he dismounted. Adah, with every dimple playing in ecstacy to her smiles, threw her white arms around his war-stained breast and kissed him. Startled and astonished at his coldness, for he indeed stood a monument of dumb, cold despair, she exclaimed, "My father, my father, what is it, and what has thy Adah done in thy sight that she is not welcomed?" Then, indeed, the fountains of feeling were pierced and a way was opened for words;

the warrior who had just stood a man of iron at
the head of a great army, had seen men fall beneath
his sword like grain before the reaper, and been
unmoved, now shook like a reed swayed by the
wind, and was bathed in tears; as the granite rock
is baptized by the fountain that bursts from its own
bosom. Suddenly he had been translated from the
highest elevation of joy to the deepest dejection of
despair.

Adah, appalled at this great demonstration of
sorrow, knelt at his feet, clasped his blood-stained
knees, and cried again, "My father, why is this?"
Then he answered her, "Alas, my daughter, thou
hast brought me very low, and thou art one of them
that trouble me; for I have opened my mouth unto
the Lord and I cannot go back."

Stupefied for a moment, stunned, bewildered,
horrified, Adah contemplated her father; then,
seeming to realize it all, to understand the nature
of the Israelitish vows, she slowly let her hands
droop, closed her eyes, and seemed to pray. After
that the *woman* prevailed; she thought of the sufferings of her father, her lover, and she put

aside her sorrow for herself, and stood strong to bear *their* grief. So natural is it for womanhood to *give*, to *bestow* at its *own* cost, that to many women sacrifice is sweeter than favor; there are some women of *this* day who live martyrs, and who are so comforted under the infliction that they would hardly accept release if it were offered. It was after woman's nature for Adah to look up almost cheerfully and answer, " My father, if thou hast opened thy mouth unto the Lord, do to me according to that which hath proceeded out of thy mouth; forasmuch as the Lord hath taken vengeance for thee of thine enemies, even of the children of Ammon, let *this* thing be done for me; let me alone for two months, that I may go up and down upon the mountains, and bewail my virginity, I and my maidens."

This was all she asked, she made no other requirements, plead for nothing, urged no entreaties, used no reproaches, but only stipulated for two months longer of her sweet, fresh, beautiful life. Her lover asked nothing but that he might hold her to his heart once more and die; it seemed

---

that heaven heard his prayer, for we are told that
his great grief induced fatal disease and caused his
speedy death.

We would fain close our history, would fold over
the terrible tragedy, sublime in its very horror, a
veil, but our readers call for the whole drama, and
we set our face hard and follow Adah to the seclusion
of her mountain retreat, whither she had repaired
to do penance and sanctify herself for her sacrifice.

We know that there are doubts about the actual
fulfillment, to the letter, of Jephthah's vow. To be
deprived of the joys of connubiality and condemned
to perpetual virginity was to the Jews a great affliction, disgrace, and punishment; whereas to the
Catholics, *vice versa*, it is an honor, and the surest
means of securing divine favor.

It is allowed by some that Jephthah might have
fulfilled his vow so far. But assuming that no com-
mutation of the full sentence was made, Adah was
offered and slain; her flesh burned with fire, and
the incense of the offering arose to His nostrils and
was acceptable, according to the Israelitish faith, to
the Lord God Almighty.

As another has forcibly illustrated the closing scene, we quote him, glad to escape the thrilling torture of describing the offering of so vital a thing as human life for a sacrificial spectacle.

"When the two months had expired, and the day arrived which was to bring this sad affair to a close, a vast multitude gathered together to witness the event. Precisely as the sun came on the meridian, she was seen, followed by a long train of her friends, wending her way down the mountain's side to the fatal spot where the altar was erected, and her father, with an almost broken heart, was standing, prepared to fulfill his vow. She approached him, and with one long kiss of affection bade him farewell. Taking hold of the thick mourning-veil which she wore, he drew it gently over her face and drew his sword. But she rapidly unveiled herself, and said she needed not to have her face covered, *for she was not afraid to die.* Her father replied that he could not strike the blow while she looked upon him, and again cast it over her. She threw it off the second time, and, turning from him, said she would look up to the heavens so that his hand should not be unnerved by the sight of her face, but that *she would not consent to die in the dark.* A third time, however, he insisted, and a third time she as resolutely cast it off, this time holding the ends of it firmly in her hands, and then, in the hearing of the multitude, she solemnly declared that if this ceremony was insisted upon she would claim the protection of the law and refuse the fate she was otherwise willing to endure.

"She said it was the practice to cover the faces of murderers and criminals when they were about to be put to death, but for her part *she was no criminal, and died only to redeem her father's honor.* Again she averred that she would cast her eyes upward upon the Source of Light, and in that position she invited the fatal blow. It fell."

We are glad that the curtain has shut out the tragedy, and that we may hopefully raise it again upon heaven, where our sanctified, redeemed heroine has met her *Andra,* has looked upon *motive,* seen *cause,* and realized *consequence.*

Jephthah after this became sanctified to the Lord. He judged Israel for six years, and was

"gathered to his fathers." His piety is historical.
.His words have passed down successive generations
as oracles. And all the years of his latter life ex-
piated the offences of his youth.

In Adah's life we find a truth
　　Which every woman knows,
That virtue, planted in one's youth,
　　Through all one's future grows;

That modesty will throw a grace
　　O'er genius, and devise
A model for the highest place
　　Among the good and wise.

That beauty is a goodly thing,
　　If coupled with desire
To lift the intellect, and bring
　　Genius and wisdom nigher.

That sweet humility which craves
　　No more than it deserves
Shuts off much cruel grief, and paves
　　A path which it *preserves.*

Though riches flow to magic touch,
　　And high position buy,
Yet woman knows that nothing such
　　Her heart can satisfy.

3*

A meek and quiet spirit sees
In humblest lot a peace,
And circumstance of wealth and ease
Her joy cannot increase.

To bend one's spirit low beneath
The yoke of duty, may
Fix on one's brow the victor's wreath
In some far future day.

The patient service of true good
Through industry and might,
By power supreme is understood
And to the end worked right.

THE TOPAZ IN THE FIELD OF BOAZ.

II.

The Topaz.

RUTH.

HUMAN circumstances create themselves; in various tones, coloring, and phase, they blend until the universal groundwork or actuality is only a repetition of the minor parts. The relation of cause with effect, the likeness of human passions, the correspondence of human interests, all compare equally, and assert that man is liable to be controlled by the same principles; and whether he loses or gains, he will still be influenced by the power of thinking. Dates, periods, and epochs alter, but principles never.

Truth is as immortal as God, and when applied to things, is as immutable.

In one essential point, throughout all ages, nations, and places of the world, however different in character, inclination, and manner, men are united—the inherent recognition of, and adoration for, a Supreme Power, and they have devised external manner to demonstrate their faith, and declared openly their dependence upon it.

Religious sentiment, enthusiastically followed, has originated some of the greatest designs in every art that science ever knew; has dictated the most severe virtue, and fulfilled the most holy obligations of filial piety, records of which may be had from the infancy of the world to the present day, this century repeating the principle that the first declared.

To the heathen as well as to the Jew and Gentile, this manifestation is alike given, and we cannot more forcibly illustrate its practical application than in a recital of the life and character of the beautiful Scripture heroine RUTH.

This young woman of Moab was reared amid all the comforts that wealth can secure. She was ten-

derly and delicately nurtured; was accustomed to
wear *scarlet* and *purple*, which could not be obtained
except at great expense, and the fact of a person's
wearing these colors was a proof of high position
and title to great riches. She was of an idolatrous
race and nation, and zealously observed all the
feasts that her religion required. These feasts were
numerous.

The most particular one was Eleusis, or "The
Mysteries," into which parents were particularly
careful to initiate their children at an early age,
because the ceremony made a compact which
secured the protection of the goddess to whose services they dedicated themselves, and was the means
of a more perfect and happier life in the future.

We may very readily suppose that it was at this
feast that Mahlon, the Hebrew stranger lately come
to Moab, for the first time saw Ruth, and we may
naturally draw the picture of their meeting.

Upon the evening of the fourth day during the
feast, the Procession of the Basket took place. An
immense basket, elegantly designed and decorated,
was laid upon an open chariot, and, slowly drawn by

oxen, was followed by numbers of women, all of whom carried mysterious baskets in their hands, filled with articles that they took great pains to conceal.

As Mahlon stood under an arch, or in an embrasure, curiously observing this ceremony of the idolaters, his attention became suddenly riveted upon Ruth, who, in her anxiety to conceal the contents of her basket, paused a moment behind the others to arrange the elegant covering of embroidered silk over her mysteries; her hands, like two sensitive lilies, were cunningly and dexterously fastening the top.

Her hair, which was of shiny black, luxuriant and soft, was waved freely back from a broad, pure brow.   Her eyes, of liquid black touched by diamond glints, were raised as if by some potent mysterious agency, and caught for one moment the gaze of Mahlon.   The telegram of love instituted the initiatory of the union of two races which was finally to create the house of David, the beloved of the Lord.

Elimelech, a man of distinction, rich and influen-

tial, was a Jew of the tribe of Judah. He lived,
honored and respected, with Naomi, his wife, and
two sons, Chilion and Mahlon, until he was past
middle life, in Bethlehem-Judah, or Ephratah,
which was his native place. In consequence of a
famine which devastated the land, he removed his
family to Moab, where both of his sons married
Moabitish women, Ruth and Orpah. Such unions
were contrary to the given law of the Lord.

In the case of Ruth, her devotion to Mahlon, her
husband, overcame every prejudice; the God that
he worshipped became her God, and whatever constituted his happiness created her joy and satisfaction. What he desired she desired, and she was
converted from idolatrous worship to the Hebrew
religion. She was devoted to her husband; loved
him with all the earnestness of a first genuine affection, and with all the strength that a character so
tender, yet so strong as Ruth's, was capable of. In
the poetic version of Scripture phraseology she
proved that "She will do him good and not evil all
the days of her life," and that "A good wife is from
the Lord."

After a few years of joyous wedded life, Mahlon died and also Chilion. Elimelech, too, was dead. When Mahlon lay upon his deathbed he charged Ruth not to forsake her adopted religion, but after he was buried, to cleave to it still through every chance and change.

Great was the sorrow of the lovely young widow, when she was left by her best beloved to tread the path of life alone; it is not surprising that she should cling to her who was her Mahlon's mother; and though the riches of Elimelech, with which he came full-handed, were all exhausted, and the three widows, Naomi, the mother-in-law, and her two daughters-in-law, Orpah and Ruth, were very poor, and were barely supplied with necessary comforts, yet they would not separate, but with tenacious constancy remained under the same roof, each contributing her small share of earnings to fill the meagre exchequer's daily demand, thus fulfilling the law of affection to its strictest letter.

The hour of adversity brought out the genuine goodness, portrayed each characteristic, and developed the strongest points in the disposition of

Ruth. Her own relations were wealthy and extended the most earnest solicitations for her to come and share with them their comfortable home and appointments, but the faithful heart looked through the dim obscurity of the grave up to heaven, where was her beloved, who held her registered vow. She refused every invitation and abode with Naomi; and with her own delicate hands performed chief part of the menial duties.

· Orpah, seeing the example of Ruth, emulated her, but when poverty pinched her sorely she had secret longings for the ease which competence insures, and which was within her reach, and when Naomi urged her to leave her she was scarcely strong enough to resist the temptation; but she really loved Naomi, and would have been willing to stay with her forever if such a course had not involved her personal comfort. To make self-sacrifice was not her prevailing quality, but a love of ease was.

Things became worse and worse in the little household; it was hard to live, and Naomi became greatly depressed, and determined to return to her early home if it were but to die and to have a place

to be buried in ; she longed to be where she could
enjoy her religious rites and ceremonies, and believed that by retracing her way back from her
weary stay in a foreign land, the God of her forefathers would approve the act, for she had violated,
through her husband's will, the law which forbids a
chosen one to go, of his own will and inclination, to
dwell with the heathen. This act of disobedience
she firmly believed had brought ill consequences :
her present forlorn condition.

She and Ruth and Orpah set out on foot; a " far
journey," as it was then called, owing to imperfect
navigation and slow modes of land-travel. The
flowers were in full bloom, the grape-blossoms
scented the air, the birds sang their thanksgiving
hymns, and even the little fishes that swam hither
and thither in the brooks that they passed seemed
to rejoice, and to appeal to them to look up to the
great source of all love for a renewal of their happiness. After they had travelled a few miles
Naomi's spirit became depressed, her steps faltered,
and she seemed to realize the hardships which
they should have to encounter before they could

reach the end of their toilsome journey, and her
kind heart refused to involve in this trouble her two
daughters.

She threw herself down on the green sward, her
garments trailed among the sweet wild anemones,
and her brow pressed the rich tufts of lobelia, while
her hands tremulously clasped Ruth's and Orpah's;
her voice rose above the murmur of the brook that
ran close beside the pathway, as she in earnest
tones begged her daughters-in-law to return to their
friends: to leave her to pursue her way alone; if
she perished, it would be only an old woman, without any relative to mourn her, who died; but that
they were young, with many years before them, with
numerous friends whose hearts would be gladdened
by their society.

In her breast mingled emotions contended for
mastery. To part with them, Ruth especially, was
as terrible as death. It was a dreadful thought to
be left *alone* at her time of life; very sweet to realize
that a tender solicitude was felt for her, and to retain this blessing was of course the first wish of her
heart; but her generous mind craved their happi-

ness, and she feared that they would realize the reverse if they stayed by her.

Suddenly she raised her eyes to theirs and impressively pointed out to them, in eloquent words, the advantage to be gained by a return home, and the privations and discomfort which would follow them if they remained with her. She endeavored to persuade them to pursue the first course. Ruth twined her arms around Naomi and uttered the most eloquent chapter of love that has ever been spoken, in these words : " Entreat me not to leave thee or to return from following thee. Whither thou goest I will go ; and where thou lodgest I will lodge. Thy people shall be my people, and thy God my God. Where thou diest I will die, and there will I be buried. The Lord do so to me and more also, if aught but death part thee and me !"

No studied oration could have expressed more undying, changeless, self-forgetting devotion than these simple words. Naomi's heart bowed in admiration for so sublime a manifestation.

Orpah loved Naomi and kissed her repeatedly,

and was anxious to manifest her love, but her fond-
ness for self-indulgence and dread of the prospect
of poverty in a strange land prevailed, and, with
many tears, though with some secret relief, she bade
adieu to her two companions and retraced her steps.

Naomi no longer opposed Ruth's determination ;
it would have been an insult to human affection ;
but she rose from the ground upon which she had
thrown herself, renewed and strengthened to resume
her journey.   Ruth sang as they walked, and whenever they stopped to rest brought wreaths of wild
flowers and playfully twined them around Naomi's
waist and wrists, endeavoring by every little art to
wile her thoughts from the difficulties of their route.

At last, tired, dusty, travel-stained, and hungry,
they entered the gates of Bethlehem.   It is due to
the people of the times to say that the warm sympathy shown to Naomi on her arrival proved them to
be unselfish enough to spare both feeling and time
for their returned countrywoman, and to grieve with
her at those heavy afflictions which caused her to
reply to their eager questions, " Call me not Naomi,
the pleasant, the sweet, but Mara, the bitter, for the

Almighty hath dealt very bitterly with me. I went
out full and the Lord hath brought me home again
empty. Why, then, call ye me Naomi, seeing that
the Lord hath testified against me, and the Almighty
hath afflicted me."

The poetical interpretation of the name Naomi is
pleasantness, sweetness, grace. Bitterness and sad-
ness were now more applicable to her, and she
plaintively reminded her friends of the fact. She
did not mean to complain, but to prevent them from
recurring to the past, which afforded such contrast
with her present condition. Her friends would have
heaped favors upon her and the gentle Ruth, who
modestly remained silent and retiring, but Naomi
could not bear to become an object of pity, and so
with their small means they secured a very humble
dwelling in the suburbs, and she and Ruth commenced their frugal life in Naomi's native city.

Curiosity dictated no idle inquiries about Ruth;
the Israelites were too well versed in politeness to
stare or to ask questions; but many a furtive glance
was given, and whispered expressions of admiration
were made at her exceeding loveliness. She was

divested of purple, and blue, and scarlet colors, the insignia of wealth and consequence, now, and was simply robed in pure white linen, with a hood of the same over her head, and half sandals upon her feet.

When they arrived at Bethlehem it was the time of barley harvest. Naomi had a very wealthy relation of the family of Elimelech, who, according to Jewish law, was bound to provide her with all the relief that she needed, but her unassuming disposition led her to prefer for the present to remain in retirement, because the contrast in their respective positions was too great. She concealed from Ruth his existence.

It was customary for the peasantry to be allowed to pick up the grain they might find which had been left upon the field, and so the sacred history tells us that "Ruth went to glean in the fields, and that it was her hap to light on a part of the field belonging to Boaz." If Ruth had known of this connection she would have hesitated to work at this place, but as she was ignorant of it, of course she was rejoiced to be so near home, and was glad to find Boaz so conciliatory to *her*, who was a stranger, and had no

4

right to presume upon the privilege of the Jewish
women.

Boaz observed her modest deportment, and also
her elastic figure, which was the very embodiment
of grace and beauty, as she industriously performed
her tasks, and he told her that it was not necessary
for her to go into any field but his, and to stay by
his maidens. He told her also to keep close after
the reapers, for that she should not be insulted or
ill-treated.

How grateful this act of appreciation must have
been to the sensitive young widow no one can
realize but she who has also been a stranger in a
strange place, performing offices which threw her
under a light totally different from that of her usual
sphere, and which subjected her in a measure to
coarse treatment. With the sweet candor and gentle humility of her nature, she, knowing that from
her present position she would not seem to be
entitled to such consideration, inquired of Boaz:
"Why have I found grace in thy eyes that thou
shouldst take this knowledge of me, seeing I am a
stranger?"

Honest praise is very gratifying, and has often
given an impetus to a heart for a renewal of effort,
which had nearly sunk under misappreciation. The
meed of well-earned approbation which the answer
of Boaz conveyed, was joyfully received by Ruth ;
her mind delighted to find that she, through virtuous conduct, had secured a friend, possibly, for herself, and her countenance lighted up by the reflection of these pleasant thoughts. Boaz, taking the
covering from his head, bent respectfully forward,
and, looking upon her sweet downcast eyes, said
with serious impressiveness : "It hath been fully
shown me all that thou hast done unto thy mother-
in-law since the death of thine husband ; how thou
hast left father and mother, and the land of thy
nativity, and art come unto a people which thou
knewest not heretofore. The Lord recompense thy
work, and a full reward be given thee of the Lord
God of Israel, under whose wings thou art come to
trust."

There was such unmistakable respect, and tender
interest besides, intimated by his manner, that
Ruth's heart trembled with satisfaction, tears sprang

to her eyes, and so much sensibility manifested itself in her voice as she answered, "Let me still find favor in thy sight, for thou hast spoken friendly to thy hand-maid, though I be not like one of thine own hand-maidens," that Boaz was betrayed into an emotion of tenderness which he could not suppress.

He turned suddenly away, lest he should betray the peculiar interest that he felt toward the strange serving-woman, which would make him seem to his dependants to be taking undue familiarity. But at dinner he seated her near to himself, and waited upon her, for it is said that he handed her the parched corn. A beautiful picture the fair-skinned Moabitess seated among her olive-skinned companions must have presented; a most novel and pleasing sight, indeed; so delicate, with the evident and unmistakable signs of high birth and breeding depicted in the countenance, in the hand; her peculiar distinction from her companions by the manner of handling her spoon; the attention bestowed upon her by her landlord, all set forth a contrast which was unmistakably interesting.

There was a distinguishing refinement about her

which made her the especial figure in the scene,
and the young men all held her in the most virtuous
esteem; they had perceived that she was entitled to
their profoundest respect.

Boaz urged his hospitality, and was pleased to
see her partake with a good appetite of the viands
set before her; and when she had concluded her
dinner he followed the young men, or reapers, and
ordered them to drop some of the sheaves so that
she might have a plenty to take home with her.
This was a favor which the reapers most willingly
accorded, for each one was impressed with the
superiority of the beautiful stranger. Ruth was
industrious, and gathered enough to make an ephah
of barley.

Naomi had felt some anxiety about this now
doubly-dear child of her adoption, and often, as the
sun got low, she had gone to the door to look if she
was coming. When at last Ruth came into the
doorway, her face lighted up with the pleasant news
she had to impart, Naomi's affectionate heart was
stirred with joy; she herself brought cool water and
refreshed Ruth with it, then made haste to bring

some choice dish of food which she had saved for her, affectionately asking questions of her, whilst Ruth ingenuously described the marked respect she had received from Boaz.

Naomi was astonished when she heard the name of Boaz, and she ascribed it to no mere chance that Ruth had been guided to him. She was constrained to give expression to her gratification, and she cried, "Blessed be the Lord who hath not left off his kindness to the living and the dead." She imparted to Ruth their near relationship to Boaz, and commended her for her observance of all he had told her; and so, on the morrow, Ruth repaired again to the same field, where she met with fresh kindness.

It was not a mere speculation, or love of matchmaking, which induced Naomi to set about scheming for a union between Ruth and Boaz, but the tender, devoted love of a mother, who, knowing well the excellence of Boaz, was anxious to secure the happiness to her daughter which her marriage to him might secure.

The warmth of her heart centred on this daughter, who had by every act manifested for herself the most undèviating devotion. It is well said that a dutiful daughter always makes the most perfect wife; this Naomi had seen proven, for as a wife to her son, Ruth had fulfilled the most strict minutiæ of duty and devotion, had made his heart glad throughout the whole ten years of their married lives.

Naomi, understanding what the Jewish law was, determined to use those means which, under God's especial providence, might result in so much benefit to all. Naomi trusted in God. Through every vicissitude of ill luck or prosperity, she had never ceased to supplicate and to praise; and she had laid up a store of peace and joy, through this means, for her old age; her mind was placid, and rested content with the assurance of God's everlasting protection.

Pious beauties mellowed by time assume a fervid lustre. Patient endurances had shed a calm, steady light throughout Naomi's soul, which no circumstance of misfortune or poverty could obscure. But she deemed it her duty to embrace the means presented for the benefit and comfort of her daughter, who was so deserving and who was yet so young; and she gave instructions to Ruth which at first seemed very revolting to the Moabitess, for there was no such rule among her own people; her modesty and strict sense of propriety were shocked; but as she had known Naomi for so long, as kind as her own mother, and had perfect faith in her prudence, she consented to abide by whatever she might tell her, and she simply answered: "All that thou sayest unto me that will I do."

It was the custom of the Jews when a marriage was contemplated between near relatives, or with the widow of a deceased relative, for the female to steal in the night-time to the feet of the man and lay herself down, drawing the coverlid over her; this was a significant sign for him to extend the mantle of protection, or was an opportunity for her to ask, "Give me thy protection as a husband."

Judging men by common rules, we conclude that it is no mean proof of chivalry for a man to exercise his discretion so far as to show no immodest or indecorous behavior towards a beautiful woman who lies at his feet. To insure confidence is to give confidence, and the mere act of a woman's passively submitting herself to the peculiar situation may possibly arouse the man's most beautiful sentiment of honor and generosity.

"In the midst of the night," as Naomi instructed Ruth to do, she repaired to the sleeping apartment of Boaz, with what trepidation any modest mind may conceive, and laid herself down at his feet.

Her beautiful figure palpitated with contending emotions; the soft moonlight streaming in and falling on her face, exposed its paleness. She lay trembling like an aspen-leaf controlled by the breeze, until Boaz, awaking in alarm, perceived who she was, knew that she was acting in exact accordance with the law, and reproved her not, but spoke encouragingly and pleasantly to her, which so reassured Ruth that she talked freely to him of some facts in her life and history.

The heart of Boaz was in his hand, and willingly enough he drew his mantle or covering over his beautiful charge and assured her of his willingness to become her husband, and the high honor he felt she would be conferring upon him. But there was one shadow which clouded the atmosphere of his

J *

anticipations, the fact that there was a nearer relative, still, than himself, who, according to Jewish law, had a stronger claim to her than he had.

Ruth's heart was still with her dead Mahlon, and she cherished his memory most tenderly; but she was discreet as well as affectionate, and she judged that to do what her mother-in-law advised was a proper rule to go by, and she assumed no prudery nor affected any sentimentalism which might reflect pain or ill consequences to one so dear. She had had opportunity of observing the high tone of disposition and conduct of Boaz, and his present generous behavior toward herself was not without its softening tendency.

Boaz pledged his word to marry Ruth if the other kinsman did not enforce his claim, and took tender care of her till the morning, when, careful for her reputation, he awakened her before it was light enough to distinguish one person from another, and, after having filled her veil with barley, showed her the secret way out. Naomi nervously awaited the result of the interview, anxious for Boaz to be the bridegroom instead of the other kinsman.

The gate of the city was the place for the transaction of all magisterial business. People of every class and grade were accustomed to assemble there, and when one wished to inquire for or to find another, the gate was the safest chance wherein to look. Boaz found this other relative of Naomi's there, and made known to him the business of Naomi and Ruth.

This relative, owing to some nice technicality, could not properly become the husband of Ruth, but he bought Naomi's claim to a field of ground and transferred his right of husband to Boaz.

With joy irradiating his countenance, his heart beating in time to his happy thoughts, Boaz repaired to Naomi's house, related the result of his interview with the kinsman, and handed over to her her just inheritance, the money for her land. Naomi kissed him, fell upon his neck and wept for very joy.

Sweet must have been this realization of her fond hopes for the success and prosperity of her beloved Ruth, and she praised the Lord that he had done. her so much good now that the hairs of her head were all white and her life was in its sear leaf.

She feelingly related to her cousin how faithfully
Ruth had acted toward her. She described the
various evidences of her noble, virtuous, and constant nature, displayed in the different relations of
life and departments of social obligation. First she
spoke of her, a young girl of heathenish religion,
her chaste regard of outward proprieties; she told
him that though Ruth's parents would have indulged any extravagant whim, yet she never presumed upon their generosity to extort extra jewels
or articles of dress; that she ran into no excesses
which some of the ceremonies belonging to their
feasts justified.

She then descanted upon her virtues as a wife;
how she had, immediately on her marriage to
Mahlon, embraced his religion; for his sake had
stood the scorn of her teachers; had made his faith
her faith, its practices her pleasure, and thus
secured a double bond between them. In all of her
wifely duties she had displayed the most cheerful
acquiescence, the keenest discrimination, and the
most ingenious economy.

Naomi told Boaz all this and more of the perfec-

tions of Ruth. She descanted upon her conduct
under adversity when affliction and poverty assailed
Mahlon, when all the manifold tribulations of re-
verses were heaped upon his head. When every
vestige of property was swept off, and day by day
they became poorer, Ruth never uttered a word of
complaint or repined at the personal discomfort to
which she was subjected, but was ever cheerful, and
gave to the meagre aspect of their humbled home a
general glory by her consistent good-temper and
easy adaptation of herself to the circumstance of
the hour and her ready expediency in averting an-
noyances.

When Mahlon's anxiety for an heir increased, she
with patient sweetness reminded him, from his own
scriptural history, of Sara, who had a child in her
old age, playfully suggesting that when they became
wiser God would give them children. Naomi said
she knew that Ruth's barrenness had been a source
of private mortification to her, but that she had
never sought to cast the fault upon her husband, or
complained of injustice from God.

Naomi told Boaz of the untiring fidelity of Ruth

to her husband during his long illness; of the
sacred reverence with which she bowed her head to
Almighty God under the terrible dispensation of his
death, and of her inimitable devotion and beautiful
deportment to herself since she was made a widow;
and declared that Ruth fulfilled to the letter
another proverb: "The heart of her husband doth
safely trust in her so that he shall have no need of
spoil."

The heart of Boaz swelled with delightful emotions at this description of Ruth's perfections, and
his fine face, beautiful in shape and feature, glowed
with the reflection of genuine appreciation. Love
controlled him, and the god painted his image in his
eyes when, at the close of Naomi's speech, Ruth,
unexpectedly appearing, beheld him.

Bashful still and timid, she sensitively shrunk
back, as a rose beneath the full glare of the sun,
made a reverence, and was about to retire, when
Naomi called to her and said, "Nay, my daughter,
thou needest not be shamefaced, but come forward
and receive the hand of him who is to be thy husband;" and Ruth, with the simplicity of perfect

obedience which she always accorded to her mother-
in-law, did as she was requested, gracefully came
forward and stood before Boaz.   He extended his
hand, drew her toward him, kissed her; took a
ring and placed it upon her finger, and bestowed
many kind and affectionate assurances of his devotion and intentions for the future.

Of course she went no more into the fields, but
commenced to get ready for the celebration of her
nuptials.

Do not let our readers suppose that Ruth had
forgot Mahlon.   She could not forget what had
come into the soft, tender, springtime of her life;
his memory was indelibly printed on the walls of
her heart, and no other or more recent impression
could ever obliterate it; but as over old and great
pictures are sometimes laid fresh coats, so Ruth
took into her affections a second love, through
which the lines of the first might again be expressed.

It is so especially woman's nature to love, that
Ruth experienced the want which her husband's
death had created; the void was there, and to wish

to fill it, with as perfect representation of its first
object as was possible, was natural; she shrunk
from a lonely path, felt the necessity of a strong
arm to lean on in her weakness; and when she
realized that she was the subject of a man's love,
whom she knew to be superior in imparting
strength, consolation, and changeless sympathy; a
friend who would not forsake her, never leave her
lonely, but who would diffuse pleasure and comfort
over her path, and that through her happiness
Naomi would also be blessed, she not only accepted
Boaz cheerfully, but joyfully.

She could not forget the sensation which his first
words occasioned her, when her tender feet were
wounded by the stubble of the fields, her delicate
hands were burning beneath their unusual occupations, her pure brow scorched by the rays of the
sun, her eyes brimming with tears, her lips quiver-
ing with pent-up anxiety, and her heart sorely
oppressed with a sense of her dependence and utter
loneliness (for she was a stranger among the hand-
maidens, who were of different kind)—she could not
forget how kindly he then spoke and attended to

her wants. Words are great things when spoken
under some circumstances, and

> There's never a word that has been told
> Which, spoken through a spirit cold
> Or warm, has ever yet been lost.
> It either sighs and tears has cost,
> Smiles and pleasant fancies brought,
> Or lessons of great love has taught.
>
> A word! why 'tis as mighty as a fire
> Of great proportion; in its ire
> Burning out all the gladdest things
> That rich enthusiasm brings,
> Heaping ashes where ambition grew,
> Where hope was—leaving grief—in lieu.
>
> A word has crushed the tender bloom
> Of love; has hastened to a doom
> Obscure sweet aspiration, and
> In stifling every keen demand
> For human sympathy, has laid
> Ground for misanthropy instead.
>
> Again, a single word reversed
> Has copious streams afresh coerced,
> Toward all that fills the widest scope
> Of joy, philanthropy, and hope;

Has turned a widow's drooping weed
To consolation's richest meed;

Has crushed to atoms grim despair
And from the ruins built things rare;
Has scattered to the winds mistrust,
And wove a fabric of stanch trust;
Has harmonized, and humanized, and fed
A soul, till up to heaven 'twas led.

Words were of consequence to Ruth, for they
gave her flagging spirit a new impetus, and opened
a volume of bright thoughts where before had
merely existed the shut book of endurance. Kind
words came like dew to the parched flower, the sun
to the frozen rill, the mother's breast to the babe,
and food to the hungry.

Never before had she looked more lovely than
now. Exercise in the open air had created a rosy
bloom in her cheek, and her mouth, so purely the
index of her feelings, reflected sweet content. Her
eyes sparkled with unusual brilliancy, and her
beautifully-shaped throat seemed raised with a new
dignity.   •

Boaz proclaimed to the people, and all the

elders, the fact of his purchase of Naomi's land and of his betrothal to Ruth. He received the congratulations of all, and the elders and the people bore witness joyfully, and prayed that the Lord would make the woman whom he had chosen like Rachel and Leah, who had built up the house of Israel, and that he himself might "do worthily in Ephratah and be famous in Bethlehem." After the allotted season of waiting, Boaz and Ruth were married.

It was in the season when the fruit hung mellow with ripeness, luscious with the juices of perfectness; when the birds fledged in the spring were now matrons themselves; the lambkins that sported were nearly full grown; and the season itself felt that it had served its time, had fulfilled its part, and was ready to lay by its rich mantle of crimson and gold, and retire.

On one morning, cloudless and balmy, during the autumn, their nuptials were solemnized, and the bride fulfilled another proverb: "Strength and honor are her clothing, and she shall rejoice in time to come."

There was much feasting and rejoicing attending

the occasion. The beautiful, serene, meek-eyed Ruth was the delight of all eyes, and especially was she the joy and satisfaction of Naomi's heart, which had seen of Ruth's perfections of character, and rejoiced in her deserved reward.

Peace and plenty were again their portion, for Boaz was "A man who was mighty and rich." Naomi had apartments in his household, which Ruth delighted to adorn, and many a day of calm reflection had Naomi. She often sat at decline of day and watched the sunset gild the fields with its last lingering glance, blessing the world even as it went out; and we may liken Naomi's silver tresses scattered over the aged brow to snow upon an old-time open page; her dim eyes to windows between two worlds with veils spread upon them. Her bent figure was the living monument of human decay; her hands, still busied in some needlework, transcripts of the everlasting principle of will; and she seemed, her very self, to resemble the waning sunlight; for with her influence of perfect love and goodness she illuminated and glorified all around as she declined toward the tomb.

No studied phraseology can ever measure the estimate of true virtue; it is its own definition, and shapes its own destinies. Good works are followed by great ends, and noble action is rooted where time, nor rust, nor tempest can ever unsettle it.

The lessons that Ruth had learned in her hours of misfortune and poverty were the groundwork of deeds of charity, patient forbearance, and love, which her munificent means now enabled her to effect. Her life she determined to make a practical fulfillment of these obligations, applied as well to the most trivial as to the greatest opportunities.

She ordered her household well, and pursued with her own hands many domestic avocations, and verified still another problem: "She looketh well to the ways of her household, and eateth not the bread of idleness."

Throughout Naomi's adversity Ruth had clung to her; now Naomi clung to Ruth, and she was sought after, admired, and emulated by her husband's relations. Boaz was a fond and devoted husband, and refused nothing to Ruth and Naomi.

At last the beautiful dream was realized; the

secret sweet wish of all true women's and true
wives' minds was realized to Ruth; she had conceived; the beautiful development in her nature
was revealed; the germ which is so sacredly
wrapped in woman's organism was set to pulse, for
she felt the sweet joy that the babe was leaping in
her womb. Motherhood! 'tis the baptism of God,
the consecration of angels, and the culmination of
every perfect desire.

When the full time for her delivery was come,
and Naomi and Boaz anxiously awaited the result,
from the crisis the most joyful of sounds, an infant's
first manifestation of intelligent existence, a feeble
wail was heard, and a "man-child," it was told by
the attendants to Boaz, had been born. Ruth
thrived; the infant was called Obed, and became
grandfather to David.

Naomi took the child to her bosom, constituted
herself its nurse, and thus relieved Ruth of the
anxieties incidental to having strange nurses.
Every mother will appreciate this great favor, of
having her first child especially cared for by as
loving and more experienced hands than her own,

herself relieved of all anxiety during the perilous four weeks subsequent to parturition. A young mother is blest who has such a friend as Naomi to relieve her of the charge, one whom she can so freely trust to foster in her own bosom the young fibre of a new existence, the "baby," the mother's first-born.

How touching! how sublime! the whole history of Ruth and Naomi is throughout. The fact of the women of Israel coming to congratulate Naomi on the birth of her grandchild, and making her especial joy the common interest of all, rejoicing that "Naomi had a grandson;" the incident of their bringing evergreen to plant upon her brow, the symbol of the springing of a live branch from the old stock, was touching, and all joined in the chant: "Blessed be the Lord who hath not left thee this day without a kinsman, that his name may be famous in Israel, and he shall be unto thee a restorer of life and a nourisher of thine old age, for thy daughter-in-law, who loveth thee and who *is better to thee than seven sons*, hath borne him."

In the character of Ruth every woman of this day

---

may find volumes of excellence which they may do
well to copy. Virtue has double and triple mean-
ings, is full, running over, and exhaustless; is a
garment which may be fitted to all who will try to
wear it. Perfection is attainable, or Christ Jesus
would not have exhorted his disciples and audiences
to secure it. Constancy is like the sweet odors
pressed from scented flowers, and when applied like
Ruth's, is the incense that Heaven approves.

Industry will not only reap barley-grains, but will
garner results in the storehouse of immortality.

Love sanctifies, exalts, and completes a woman's
character, whether it is spread as a mantle of charity
for general good or is fixed in its most subtle refinement upon a worthy husband; and when, like
Ruth's, it is coupled with self-sacrifice, endurance,
and piety, will be a crown of glory, the highest gift
that can deck a man's life.

Marriage, when a true union of souls, is the perfect fulfillment of the law of unison in nature which
sympathetic qualities must fulfill.

Perfect fitness makes perfect concord, which is the
culmination of the divinest attributes in either sex,

and must create a condition of happiness which is desirable, sacred, good, and superior in delight to all other blisses.

Ruth stood among the women of her day
As one star in the milky way,
Prominent from a thousand others
Of maids and daughters, wives and mothers.

As a MAIDEN, she became her lot,
And graced her age; she ne'er forgot
That violets bloom the sweetest where
The modest shade shuts off the glare.

As DAUGHTER, she was satisfied to bend
Her will unto her mother's, nor pretend
To rule; she knew that when an angel stoops,
It is to bless the head that droops.

As SISTER, she combined the graces
Of true virtue, and as sunshine chases
Mist away, her genial temper chased
Discord; and pleasure in its stead placed.

As WIFE, all that the daughter promised
She fulfilled, and none the fact resist;
The wisest daughter makes the truest wife,
Crowns man with his best gift in life.

5

As MOTHER, the angels came and stood
About her—helped to every good.
And happy the son must be, in truth,
Whose mother patterns after Ruth.

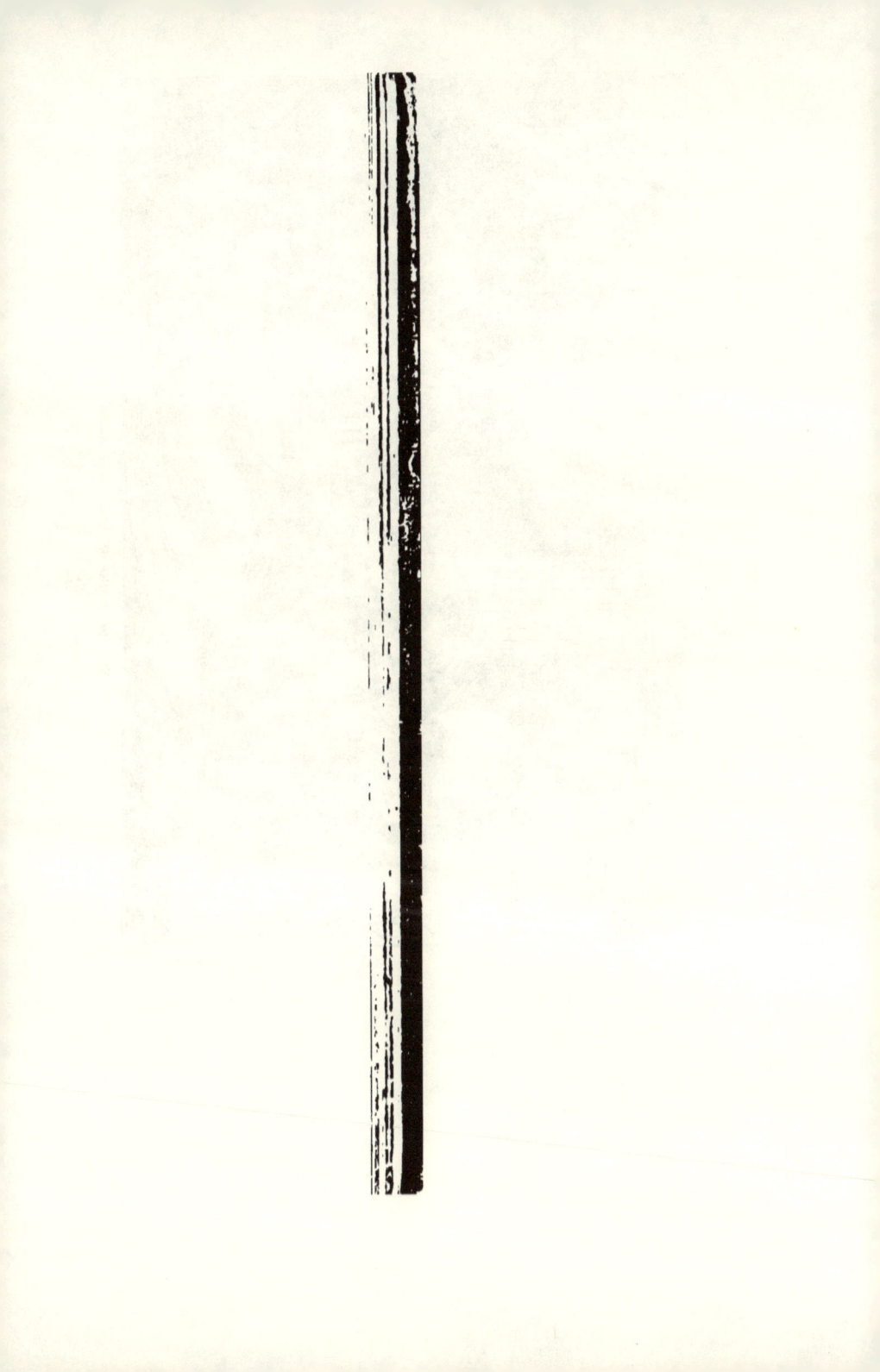

THE DIAMOND BEFORE KING AHASUERUS.

III.

The Diamond.

ESTHER.

THE Persians, a people of the acutest susceptibilities, impressional, impassioned, and enthusiastic, contemplated the beautiful through an exaggerative lens, caught from the poetical every available ray of loveliness or shadow of romance, and adorned their secular occupations with ideality and imagery.

The *beautiful* was suggested and applied in their peculiar symbolical manner to proper names, especially of females, and the name of Esther had the splendid significance of a beacon—a halo—a glory

—something which was superlative in goodness and grandeur, and its definite meaning was " A Star."

Astrologists existed amongst them, and, in the days of Artaxerxes, were famous for determining the destiny of men and women by the signs of the zodiac and the stars that governed their nativity. Through this mystical prophecy it is supposable that the fate of the Jewish maiden Hadassah was described.

Astrologers, at her birth, foretold to the anxious parents that their babe was born for high honors; that she should wear a diadem, and share the royal sceptre; that she would shine among the constellations of rank, a " star" of the first magnitude, prominent through histories of civilized and barbaric ages.

And when, years after, the significant appellative *Esther* was bestowed upon her by the Persians, it was but a continuation of the prophecy which was realized when she became the consort of Ahasuerus, the sharer of a throne.

Hadassah, a daughter of Israel, was a descendant of Benjamin, of the house of Kish, the family of Saul, who was the first king of Israel. At a tender age

she was left an orphan, and was adopted by Mordecai, a Jew of the tribe of Benjamin—one of the
ten tribes—who faithfully adhered to the house of
Judah.

He delighted to bestow all that his riches and
position could secure upon this tender bud that
he had taken to the nursery of his love; she
was reared in refinement, and also in the strictest
observance of the rites and ceremonies of the
Jewish religion. She knew no God but the great
Jehovah, the God of her forefathers. The rough
winds of hardship never assailed her, her delicate
hands were unused to a single menial service, for
she, as well as Mordecai, were of noble race, and
inherited great wealth.

During her childhood, she was designated as
"*the lovely*," on account of her gentleness and the
peculiarly amiable traits of character which she
manifested, and it was a sight which a painter
might have been proud to portray, when Mordecai,
after being fatigued with the services of the tabernacle, would bow his proud head to the shoulder
of his little charge, and drink in rest through her

sweet and intelligent prattle. At these times they sat together on a divan, his great form contrasting with her tiny figure as her little hands clasped his head against her, she assuring him that it was not too heavy, but that it was a pleasure and delight to hold it there.

The charm of her society grew with her growth and strengthened with her years. Throughout their subsequent captivity, which occurred in her early life, and through every vicissitude of trial or elation, she preserved the same cheerful obedience and willingness to serve him, and his devotion to her was very great.

She passed the usual courses of education common to Jewish maidens of rank, expanded from one perfection to another into the half-grown woman, amidst the most luxurious scenes that her high position imposed.

Mordecai, a man in whom many virtues were embodied, was of middle age when first introduced in sacred history, of fine personal appearance, and exceedingly beautiful features. He seems to have had the contrasts of qualities which are necessary

to make up the sum of the most perfect man, gentle
but firm, generous, and yielding to softness where
his finer emotions were called out, yet unflinching
in his sense of honor where duty demanded him to
be stern; humble and affectionate under justice, yet
haughty almost to scornfulness where his dignity
was insulted or his honesty impugned; loving, self-
sacrificing, fastidious yet abstemious, passionate but
temperate. An enthusiast to his religion, he recognized no heresy, and tolerated no heathen worship.

He had been constant always in his attachments,
and when he and his charge, the young Hadassah,
became exiles, and their fortunes so materially
changed that they had necessarily to live in a retired, economical manner, he became grateful to the
country of his adoption which had sheltered him,
and he preferred to remain in Persia even after
many of his expatriated countrymen had returned
to their native land.

He received his own intuitions as prophecies, and
whatever he conceived to be the will of God, delivered in this way, he unhesitatingly obeyed. Believing that the august eye of Omnipotence was
5*

reflected through his perceptions, he made every act
and event of his life one of active piety.

Purple and fine linen, beauty and luxury, had
been the conditions of their lives when Mordecai
and Hadassah came to live in Shushan, the City of
the Lilies. In the mind of the naturally refined,
contact with coarse objects, or the conditions induced by penury, must be and is disagreeable, and
no one who is versed in physiology can dispute that
externals do affect the interior or soul sense of the
individual. To the delicately-nurtured Jew and
Jewess, this reverse from affluence to penury must
have brought the usual disagreeables, inconve-
niences, and painful restrictions ; yet, like the lustre
of a genuine diamond, which, though it may be
covered with clay, still retains its brightness, their
qualities of rare virtue existed amidst the obscurity
of broken fortunes and conflicting opposites, and
their lives were glorified by the performance of
such deeds of goodness as their intrinsic merit
dictated.

At the age of twenty, Esther was a perfect model
of physical proportions, complexion, graces, and

charms, with the unmistakable expression of *soul nobility*, of virtue in its every aspect portrayed in her speaking countenance. Beautiful expression is always indispensable in glorifying the human countenance, and in this particular she was pre-eminently gifted.

Her figure, symmetrical yet somewhat voluptuous, was over medium height, her skin of that fair type of Jewish olive through which the blue vein is discernible; her eyes were pictures in which the emotions of her soul were fairly limned, changing to every shade and phase of feeling that impulse dictated. She was strangely beautiful. If we summed up all the graces of Venus and Juno, and planted them in her person, we should not be extravagant in our description.

The most beautiful of her characteristics was her piety, observed in the minutest events of every-day life; she worshipped God and conformed to the rights of her faith, so that their actual practice seemed to be the involuntary or spontaneous fitting of the work to the natural principle, the outward evidence of the inward mind.   Her religion was not a burden, but an embellishment, and was adapted as component with herself.

The *very* God was the object of her worship, and her cousin Mordecai was to her the perfect man who represented the God-qualities in human form. To all devotional minds the object which most nobly sustains the principles of its religion, exalts, by a contemplation of it, the soul up to its Author.

As all virtues exist in a truly pious woman, we with consistency sum up Esther's charms, graces, and qualities in that comprehensive term, "a truly pious woman;" and we may suppose her, from the period in her history which we next introduce, sublime enough in her character to cope with the great events incidental to the second crisis of her life, her promotion from obscurity to notoriety; strong enough to bear the adulation of a thousand, and not become vain; to mix with the rival wives of a royal husband, and yet to be superior to the weakness of jealousy and envy; to be wise enough to withstand flattery, and to bear blame.

We, in order to be clearly understood, shall have to give some account of other characters, whose

fortunes and destinies go so far toward determining events of chances and changes, precursorily to
Esther's ascension to the throne.

Shushan, the City of the Lilies, was the seat of

PERSIAN HOUSE AT SHUSHAN.

royalty; it took its poetic name from the vast quan-
tities of this beautiful flower which grew around it;
in the city, on the housetops, and everywhere that

there was room for a bulb to be planted, this graceful flower flourished.

Florists had been able to extend the species into
many varieties; the tinted, the blood-red, and the
snow-white grew also on the brink of the water, and
may have formed some part of their mythological
worships.

Shushan, as a royal residence, was like all other
similar cities of the East. It had the usual admix-
ture of pomp and penury, of gayety and pageantry,
military and civil, refinement and vulgarity. The
theatre, patronized by the king, was represented in
mimic pantomime on the street by the ballet-dancer,
singing-girl, and clown in bells and cleaver; the
august person of the king jostling the pauper; political intrigue and amours; kingly retinue, celebra-
tions of religion, which granted license to crime and
gave expiation for the same. Dice, wine, music,
the buffoon, the show, each and all were the component parts of life in Shushan.

Just the same life and occupation which have
through all ages made up the sum of existence,
have been subject to the same process of change,

undergone the different degrees of refinement and
variety of manner, incident, episode, and catastrophe, from the earliest accounts of nations up to
the present time, have been repeated and re-re-
peated at different periods, all and each completing
the requirements of their time; filling the imagination and suiting the wants of man, which, under
every dynasty, are still human.

The splendor and squalor, aristocracy and medi-
ocrity that existed in the days of Ahasuerus had
been common under other administrations, and in
the great changing panorama of men's lives and
centuric possibilities will be still and again repeated,
although mutations in public opinions and custom
sometimes overleap time, and new laws are enforced
which seem almost miraculous in development.

Throughout all barbarous or unenlightened ages
woman has been held subordinate to man; the wife
has been subject *in toto* to the will of her lord, and
her husband, whether a prophet, king, or peasant,
was in reality her master. Any attempt on her part
to resist his authority or to declare her individual
opinion was considered an outrage against the sov-

ereign authority of his will and dignity, and was
just cause for divorce, and sometimes even the
severe punishment of death.

Kings, lords, counsellors, and prophets had more
wives than one, and the king, not only having some
hundred lawfully-married wives, had also numerous
mistresses, or concubines.

Ahasuerus crowned and made queen one of his
wives, whom he placed in royal apartments and
gave maids of honor from the fair women of his
harem, who were also his wives yet not his queen.

Of course the queen's power was but nominal, and
except in her own province, the secluded apartments
of the harem, where no man but those who were
eunuchs ever went, she had no voice, and was subject to the caprices of the king; though sometimes
monarchs took to their councils their queens, and
were aided in their judicial policy by their advice.

Women of rank wore veils which effectually concealed their faces whenever they went into the
streets or public places, and on no account whatever
were they expected to reveal their features; any
such display would have been a gross violation of

the rules of modesty, and as sure an advertisement of prostitution as now it would be for a woman to parade her nude figure before the common gaze.

Only before the face of her lord dared she remove the thick covering, and reveal the charms of her eyes, the blush of her cheek, the ripeness of her lip, or the contour of her neck and arms. How particularly an object of scorn would Vashti have considered our modern belle, who, with perfect propriety, displays in the ball-room, to the indiscriminate gaze of crowds, the charms of neck and shoulders.

Our modern woman pities no more her Eastern sister who has to share the affections of one husband with many wives, than that sister would sorrow over her supposed immodesty in showing her face to any man except her husband; thus virtue or vice, modesty or the reverse, prudery or independence, are at last comparative, and are compatible or incompatible with the customs and usages of the times we live in.   .

True modesty, which shines out through the soul, is always the most desirable feature in the galaxy of woman's virtues, and is the pearl of great price, which no custom of barbaric age or of recent emancipation can sully, obliterate, or alter; and is recognizable in all colors, stages, and ages.

There is recorded that about the time of the third year of Ahasuerus, the city of Shushan was fervid with excitement in anticipation of an unsurpassed festival which would be given to the princes and nobles and to all the people, which was to last for several successive months. All of the varied paraphernalia that the coffers of the royal treasury could afford, the taste of merchants, the design of artists, and the ingenuity of the architect, were called into requisition to beautify and adorn the palace and courts, and every avenue to the royal mansion.

The result was, that never before had so gorgeous a scene been displayed in the city; purple and gold, blue and crimson, with arabesque and chased silver, lined the walls; the floors were covered with thick carpets of Persian ply in Tyrian dyes. Metallic mirrors were hung, vessels of porcelain and gold were distributed in fitting places, statues of their gods filled up niches, flowers were scattered, while such delicious music filled the corridors and halls, saloons and chambers, as deluded the senses of the guests into a foretaste of the blisses of paradise.

All that Eastern splendor and magnificence could contribute was poured in tributary streams, to aid the king in his purpose of giving the world something splendid to remember after it was over.

There is particular allusion made, in the Sacred account of this affair, to the palace gardens, in which magnificent silken tents were erected, and decorated with an extravagance and reckless disregard of expenditure which is almost fabulous; these were more particularly devoted to the gamesters, and, of course, scenes of revelry were enacted there which baffle the imagination to portray.

There is no particular reason given why this celebration was instituted—whether it commemorated a national anniversary, or that the policy of party suggested it; political intrigue, or the mere desire for pleasure, may have been, either of them, the cause; in either case it does not affect the fact that such a feast was held, which lasted several months, and that the season was replete with intoxication, debauchery, and excitement; and was followed, as is usual, by regrets, remorse of conscience, and a reproving sense of misapplied talents.

This occurred when Babylon, blood-red with riches, was filled full of the pride of pomp and power, strong in its own might, and arrogant of its possibilities.

The king entertained the men in his apartments, gardens, and pavilions; there were artificial gardens arranged on the house-tops also, which, when illuminated, made beautiful effect, and we may well imagine the perfect abandon and license of their indulgences, when we reflect that no virtuous women were present. There were women on the scene, of course, famous for their physical charms; this was an item in the programme of entertainment which was loudly applauded; but the presence of chaste ladies of refinement, which element is so potent in humanizing or allaying the gross passions, and in bringing out the charm of men's spiritual nature, was lacking, and license became lawlessness and obscenity.

But the fair women of the harem were not with-

out their share of enjoyment, the queen's apartments were also fitted in corresponding magnificence, with all the appurtenances requisite for the
entertainment of the finer tastes of the fair sex;
and the queen entertained hundreds of the daughters
of the nobility.

The rich Persian silk drapery was closely drawn
over the openings between the two departments,
which effectually separated them from the men.
Reclining on couches in elegantly-embroidered
robes, their splendid hair dressed with bouquets of
diamonds, and their tiny feet enclosed in sandals
or slippers of satin and pearls, these Peris of an
oriental clime made a parterre of exceeding beauty,
and were fit subjects for the muses to rant about.

They filled the time with innocent games, music,
dancing, and telling of tales; this last amusement
was particularly pleasing to Vashti, and the Arabian
Nights' Entertainments may be considered a fair
transcription of the stories which her maids of
honor read or recited.

When we compare the orgies of the males with
the innocent enjoyments of the females, the contrast

brings up forcibly the difference of the sexes, when
left unrestrained by the association of the other,
and we see the wisdom in the arrangement of
Almighty provision which creates the female with
the powerful prerogative of moral power, the gift of
keeping refined the fiercer, the more animalized
man.

Vashti was a woman of not only regal exterior
appointment, but was noble in soul as well; was
greatly honored and respected for her virtues and
amiability of manner, and eminently secured the
title of "hospitable hostess" during this season.

She had been greatly loved by her royal husband,
who had ever shown her the respect which her
character claimed; no indulgence consistent with
his dignity he ever refused her, and their married
lives had been uninterrupted by a single jar.

Severe and sad is our reflection upon the act of the
king which took place in the midst of this season.

One who fills the post of king for a nation should
always be the beacon of temperance and moral
worth; and repulsive to our sense of high honor is
the idea of his indulgence in degrading and obscene

exercises and habits, which puts him morally on as
low a plane as the most obscure and degraded; but
during the mad carousings of the feast which con-
tinued so long, Ahasuerus partook indiscreetly of
the various spiced wines, liqueurs, and other drinks,
and lost his dignity, became boastful of Vashti's
charms, spoke boldly and against all marital deco-
rum of their conjugal relations; and the lords and
courtiers, already half mad with the excitement of
wine, urged the king to have her brought, that all
of them might see the charms of which he boasted.

Such an act was almost unprecedented, but the
king's senses were too much obscured to reflect
upon the liberty of the nobles, and he sent to order
Vashti to come and display herself.

Imagine how her modest nature, her dignity, her
pride, must have felt outraged at such request; to
disobey, she knew was to incur any punishment that
the king's insulted authority might dictate; to obey,
was to forfeit her character as a chaste woman.

She hesitated not which to choose; and, thinking
to herself that the king would, when again sober,
possibly forgive the offence of her disobedience, if he

reflected that it was to save his honor from injury that she took the step, she refused to go, and bravely stayed.

Pale as marble and almost as fixed in position, she stood, as she gave the answer: "Tell my sovereign I pray him to excuse me."

Terrified at the second summons she stood; the elegant drapery of her royal robes trailed over her white arms around her magnificent figure, and was held up by her especial attendants. With her hands clasped together, and held supplicatingly upward, she feelingly uttered the words: "I pray you beseech my lord not to insist on an act which will cover me with shame."

Gigantic moral strength limned her chaste, exquisitely-shaped profile, when, after seeming to debate with herself a moment, one hand hanging down, the other over her heart,—a position proclaiming so forcibly the weakness of physique and the majesty of purpose,—she thought, "Come death or come divorce, I *will not sacrifice my womanhood.*"

The king's wrath was great, for it was considered a disgrace for a man, and most especially for a king, to have his word of command disregarded by his wife.

At that time if pacificatory means had been used, if his courtiers had turned the subject into another channel, and diverted his mind, he would have, when his brain was cooler, been glad that Vashti had not complied with his insulting request; but the lords declared their indignation at Vashti's disobedience, and incited Ahasuerus to a prompt divorce.

So Vashti was divorced and dethroned. With tears and much sorrow, yet with an inward conviction of having performed her duty, and a strong sense of self-approval, she left the royal palace never more to return.

When the mad excitement of the time was passed, and Ahasuerus thought over the matter, he repented him of his act, and saw the beautiful conduct of the queen in its proper light; but his decree was immutable.

The regrets, however, must have fastened upon him, and made him sad and melancholy, for the courtiers who had stimulated him to the rash act devised means for a cure to his grief; possibly they

6

were afraid that the king's indignation might fall
upon them; so it is said that they urged him to
select another wife whom he should make queen,
and the king consented.

Vashti must have been very superior, as it was
difficult to secure another woman who could compare favorably with her, and it was arranged that
all of the most beautiful virgins of the land should
be collected and pass in review before Ahasuerus; a
singular but most pleasing sight this was, as the
maidens, each one decked with all the external
arrangements which might possibly enhance their
native beauty, passed anxiously forward before the
king, awaiting his choice or rejection; and there
must have been many an ambitious maid amongst
them who longed to be chosen, and whose disappointment was great when she found herself rejected.

It is singular that Mordecai, so strict a Jew,
should have insisted upon Esther's joining in this
claim for the favor of the king's notice; it is strange
that he should have wished to marry her, against all
the rules of his faith, to one who was not of her religion, and in consideration, also, of his warm at-

tachment to his cousin, for whom many think he entertained a deeper passion than that of adopted fatherly kindness, he did not keep her in retirement, and not allow her to join the youthful procession as a candidate.

But it must have been that the prophetic meaning which he read in passing events shadowed peril to his nation, and had raised an enthusiastic zeal and prepared him to be a martyr for his country's sake, a martyr in an abandoned hope of love and joy.

In giving up Esther to the inspection of the king, the beautiful dream of his life vanished. He could have concealed her, but he urged her to go; nothing but the prophetic warnings of his mind, which predicted that through Esther there was to be deliverance from perils achieved for the Jews, could have induced him to sacrifice her to a heathen king.

Esther had never worshipped any God but the Lord God. It turned out that our sweet, gentle Hadassah pleased Ahasuerus more than any of the maidens. Her modesty in making no extravagant demands when presents were offered her, her unself-

ishness, her faultless and exquisite form could not
be resisted.

The king, as the maidens passed before him,
keenly noticed every gesture, step, and glance of
the eyes, and was particularly attracted to the dignified, easy, yet most modest and unpretentious
bearing of Esther; he perceived in her countenance
the reflection of the moral power which glorified her
whole appearance. The intellect which is clothed
by virtue and baptized in piety always imparts,
through the countenance, a sense of strength, and
Esther's face eminently reflected the divine inspiration which filled her mind.

Mordecai did not allow her to betray her parentage; his pride was great, but his love of his religion
was greater, and sufficient to overcome all things,
even the affection for Esther, which we suppose had
grown into his life.

The very effort of having to conceal from his
charge the fact of his romantic passion for her, is a
suggestion that the haughty manner he usually
observed was induced by that effort. He was too
noble to name the subject of his sentiments to her,

who he knew entertained for him only a daughter's or a sister's affection; he had crushed back the passion as a fruitless and foolish one.

How forsaken, how forlorn he must have felt, after the little lamb had been taken from its fold; the rose had been transplanted, his singing-bird caged behind the magnificent palace walls! for Esther had been taken by Hegai into the harem. The act of his resigning Esther was proof of his generous, self-sacrificing nature. It seems somewhat strange that no inquiries were instituted in regard to Esther's parentage or antecedents, but so the Scripture states.

It is not known exactly how many years elapsed between the time of Esther's adoption into the harem and her ascension to the throne; but it must have been three or four. After she had been chosen there were entertainments given in honor thereof, and then Mordecai obtained a situation under the king, but exactly what is meant by "sitting in the king's gate," it is hard to decide.

Affection for Esther must have induced him to take this step, as his reserve would hardly have courted so conspicuous a position. From his peculiarly singular place he could observe many a secret of the palace, and became a dread, possibly, on this very account, to Haman, who was an Amalekite, of an idolatrous race and nation, and who was about this same time appointed by the king as confidant, favorite, and adviser.

Mordecai discovered an intrigue against the life of Ahasuerus, and betrayed it to Esther, and thus was the means of averting so terrible a catastrophe to king and state; but, singularly enough, no reward was given to Mordecai for this benefit, but the fact was chronicled in the king's archives.

Haman was also of noble descent, or was of fine extraction as to pedigree, but, though his manners were of the most courtly cultivation, his language fluent, and his figure and whole appearance quite distinguished, yet he was wily, deceitful, and unprincipled; a schemer, seeking in all things only his own aggrandizement and the accumulation of great wealth. He gained the unlimited confidence of the king, and had great influence over him.

From the very first, Haman and Mordecai hated each other.

The hatred of their races was concentrated in and shown through the two men, and when every one was showing obsequious court to Haman, Mordecai retained his calm, proud, imperturbable manner, and made no sign or gesture of recognition, or show of respect.

When Esther was placed upon the throne, another magnificent royal feast proclaimed her triumph.

It was pleasing and flattering to the young maiden to be chosen for such high honors, and as she had no previous attachment she came sweetly and willingly to the arms of her husband, and into the favor of the king. And the king forgot Vashti in the connection, and luxuriated in the society of his bride. He could have granted her any boon.

During his honeymoon the uxorious sovereign conferred great benefits in Esther's name; the taxes of the provinces were remitted, pardons were granted to the condemned, so that Esther's name became a proverb in the land and famous in history.

She was esteemed among all the people. During this season of elevation she retained the same sweetness of manner and modest deportment, and never arrogated to herself the privileges of her high position as an excuse for scorning the humble.

The fact of her being debarred from the pleasures of participation in religious observances, in which she was so punctilious before, throws a veil of doubt over our minds whether or not she was entirely happy, though throughout every event, as the Scripture states, she preserved the same child-like obedience to her cousin Mordecai.

Esther, as it had been appointed her to become a queen and a wife, with her strict sense of duty guiding her, determined conscientiously to perform her part; and the womanly heart soon grew to love fondly and truly her lord who was so kind to her; she learned to cling to him, and created him, in the romantic book of her heart, her hero, her love.

Sadly, indeed, must it have fallen upon her, then, when the fickle, voluptuous king, growing weary of constancy, suddenly changed; his attentions declined, and finally he remained away from her altogether.

Esther was no longer the happy bride, but the sorrowful wife banished from her husband's presence. Many bitter tears did Esther shed, yet she forgot not to trust in the God of her fathers. Her attendants became devoted to her, and anything that they could offer for her consolation and amusement they did not withhold.

Splendor glittered about her, fine linen, blue and gold, flowers and music; every delectable viand which could tempt her palate was profusely spread around; yet for all these things her heart was sorrowful; for thirty days she did not behold the face of the king.

In the meantime Haman was unhappy because the despised Jew made no concessions, and not all the wealth and honor of his favored position could banish this one bitter drop from his cup. He longed for vengeance, and concocted a plan for the destruction of the whole hated race.

Mordecai secretly believed that it was through Haman's influence that the king was no longer gracious to Esther, and this fact must have made his blood boil with indignation.

6*

As he walked backward and forward before the palace gates, his serious, calm gaze riveted upon the walls behind which his beloved was, many pictures must have filled his mind of what might have been; and Esther, the star of his heart, was still in this hour, as through former years, sacred to him; for her sake he waited and watched the chances and changes, and instituted a secret surveillance over Haman, for he suspected him of double-dealing. Haman felt the suspicion through the mysterious agent, intuition, and hated him none the less for it.

Haman could not be satisfied until the astrologers were consulted about the selection of a lucky day for the slaughter of the Jews; so lots were through them cast, and, providentially for the Jews, the date was propitious for them, though it was hidden from Haman that such was the fact, and possibly even from the astrologers themselves.

According to the king's order, letters were sent into the provinces by posts, which gave the verdict of death to all; the edict ran: "To destroy, to kill, to cause to be put to death, to make perish all Jews, both young and old, little children and women, in one day."

No crime was specified, and no offer to expiate or exempt on any terms. The murder of the nation was a lawful act, the manner of destroying life was not ordered after any particular plan, but the executioners were left to their own ingenious devices to kill, in whatever way they might choose.

Every variety of torture that cold-blooded cruelty could suggest, they were at liberty to exercise ; to *exterminate* was the great end and aim. The most terrible feature in the terrible drama would be the stimulus of the promise of plunder ; each assassin would have the right to take possession of the property of his victim.

Nothing in history is more horrible to contemplate than this general massacre, which would have taken place through Haman's agency, but for the working of Almighty Providence in behalf of a chosen people. The tragedy would have instituted fresh scenes of bloodshed ; and crime and cruelty, violence and rapine, would have been the result of the terrible prelude.

All the time that these things were agitating the
people's minds, Mordecai rent his clothes, was distracted with grief, put on sackcloth and ashes, and
went through the city to condole with his distracted
countrymen who had so long lived unmolested; and
he found so much bitter woe, such helpless sorrow,
that he joined his lamentation with theirs and wept
and cried aloud.

He still preserved the same unbending reserve
toward Haman, who gathered his relatives together,
and with them talked over the subject of the
slaughter of the Jews, and with the concentrated
fires of hate and rage burning in his heart, told
them all how Mordecai had dared to treat him.

His friends advised him to get the king's per-
mission to hang Mordecai on a gallows of immense
height, and in the meantime, that it might be certainly effected, to have the gallows erected; and
Haman did so, not suspecting that he could fail to
get the king's consent to it, or to any proposition
which he might urge.

Mordecai's insignia of grief was not withheld from
the eyes of any; he made no secret of his nation.

MORDECAI AT THE PALACE GATE.

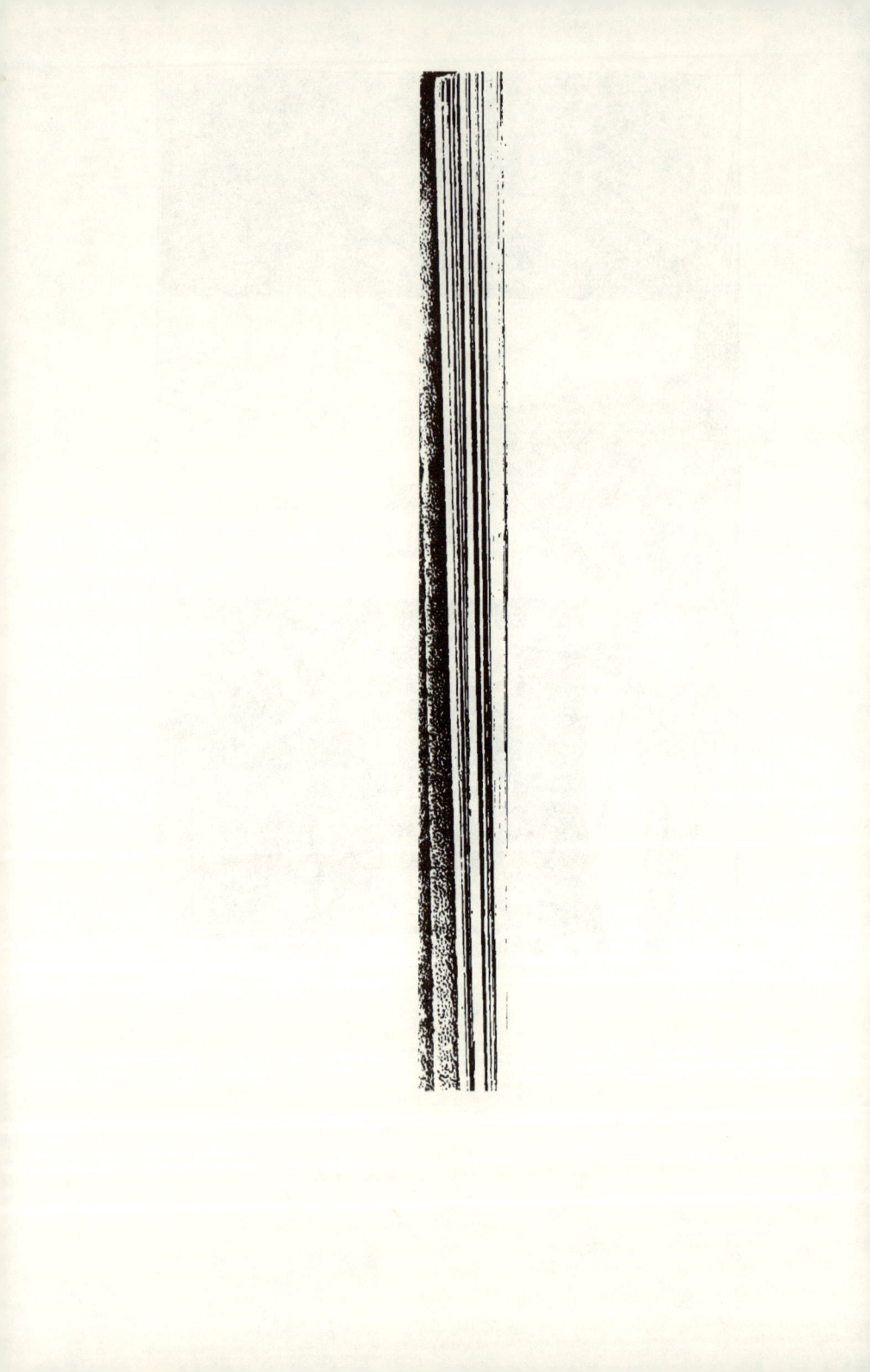

Through all the anxiety and terror he strove not to conceal that he was one of the condemned.

Ahasuerus and Haman, as usual, partook of all the pleasures of the table; wine and dice, and everything which could be brought to aid Haman in the destruction or suppression of the king's more amiable nature he called to his aid, and the king's fickleness was a tool which he used to his own aggrandizement; and while so many innocent people were plunged in the deepest grief, he must have kept the king's senses half stupefied with wine. Ahasuerus did not realize the enormity of his favorite's designs, for it is said that "Haman and the king sat down to table," the pleasures of which were intemperately appropriated, no doubt.

Mordecai must have despaired but for the prophetic whisperings of his own mind, and through the deep veil of present woe realized the light ahead. Through Esther, the star, he contemplated deliverance for his oppressed race.

This dream of joy that had come into his earlier life, the flower in his garden, the sunbeam in his house, the bird in his nest, the lamb in his fold,

the child under his roof-tree, the genius of his life,
and the deliverer of Israel; she was the means,
under Providence, to which he looked for help.

But where was Esther during this time of tribula-
tion to Mordecai and all the Jews? Unconscious
of any trouble besides that in her own heart, she
performed her duties, and fulfilled the plans of each
day with quiet dignity. She concealed her regrets
from her companions as well as she could, for her
pride was sensitive, and she would not allow any to
remark on the king's estrangement.

She gained daily and hourly the affections of all
those about her—sweet flower, the violet in retirement, which had so lately been the lily worn on a
monarch's bosom.

Esther had one sorrow which was hard to bear;
she had no communication with her own people,
and had no opportunity of observing the ceremonies of her own religion. This, to one so strictly
trained to observe these laws, was doubtless a
source of trial.

On a bright day Esther reclined on a couch of
royal velvet fringed with pearls, her robes of blue

and gold floated over her feet; the sweet perfume from a magnificent white lily, which one of her beautiful maidens had just presented to her, wafted to her senses a reminder of her humble home in Shushan before she was queen; the scenes of her peaceful life, when she cultivated her own lilies, and was content with her seclusion, and she silently begged the God of her fathers to bless her with a spirit of true submission to any trial which might assail her, but that He might not afflict her cousin Mordecai.

Judge of her distress, then, when at this moment her chamberlain reported to her an account of Mordecai's condition of grief, and repeated the edict of the king.

Like one awakened from a dream, she was at first bewildered, and her earliest impulse was to send a message or an order to him to put aside the signs of his nativity, and get out of the way of vengeance; but of course Mordecai would not obey the order, and Esther realized that she was impotent to help, and was herself involved in her nation's danger.

She knew not how she stood with the king, for

she had not seen him for many weeks. She had longed for a message or a look of love, and the royal favor seemed past. She was afraid that she was indeed forgotten; her magnificent halls, parlors, bed-chambers, with all the glitter that money and power gathered, were but prisons; her lord seemed to be the means of her torture.

She did not even know but that her place in his affections might have been filled by a later favorite; yet with all this doubt, this dark uncertainty, the dread spread before her, her noble soul, true to its instincts, looked up to a higher source, a stronger arm for help, and through faith in God's promises rose sufficient to meet the emergency.

The charms of her glittering surroundings, fairylike in beauty and appointment, had no power to rivet her regard whilst her people, and possibly herself, were in such imminent peril. She suddenly decided to go in person, unasked, and to beg with all her eloquence and earnestness that he would revoke the sentence he had passed.

She had a keen sense of her own duty, and the obligations of her religion, and she also possessed

the key to the king's mind; she knew that his
senses were susceptible to beauty, and she conceived the idea of first charming him by her fascinations into reconciliation and clemency. There
must have been a direct inspiration which dictated
her heroic resolve :

" I will go to the king, and if I perish, I perish."

Such a strong purpose, such lofty resolves, could
not have been spoken in more forcible language ;
no long sentences could have conveyed as much
emphasis as these simple words.

A devout believer in prayer, she instituted a
solemn fast of three days, in which all the Jews of
Shushan should bow themselves, and pray also for
her, before the God of their fathers. This order
was observed, not in outward celebration, but in
fervent aspiration and personal humbling of each
soul.

The queen and her maidens fasted in their secluded
portion of the palace, and the fair form, graceful
neck, and beautiful head of Esther were bowed in
the attitude of devotion and reverence which true
earnestness and perfect faith can alone dictate.

What a contrast to the crowned queen of a few
months previously! the flattered, the adored wife of
a king, decked with the adornments of majesty,
held to the breast of a devoted husband, petted,
caressed, admired, and honored, now, forsaken; with
all this grievous weight of anxiety resting upon her
heart; the orange flowers, the bridal robe, the
jewels, exchanged for sackcloth and ashes.

This was the time to try the true force of her
great nature, and to prove her heroism, faith, virtuous principle, and self-reliance. With these attributes the simple woman may be majestic in her
own beautiful womanhood, whether she be queen or
peasant.

In the meantime, Mordecai contrived private in-
terviews, in which he forcibly urged her compliance
with his request to persuade the king to repeal his
cruel sentence.

It seems to us that the Jew, Mordecai, failed at
this time to realize the true nature of Esther, her
generous, self-sacrificing spirit, for he continually
reminded her that if the nation was destroyed *she*
could not escape; which injunction implied a possi-

bility of her being selfish enough to secure her own safety, without making an effort for her people.

He said to her: "Think not with thyself that thou shalt escape in the king's house more than all the Jews, for if thou altogether holdest thy peace at this time then shall there deliverance arise to the Jews from another place, but thou and thy father's house shall be destroyed; and who knoweth whether thou art come to the kingdom for such a time as this."

This suspicion of infidelity must have pained our sensitive Esther, unless she reasoned that Mordecai supposed the mind of his Hadassah had been turned by her high position. He certainly could not have appreciated her unselfish nature, and how strong to act she could be when aroused to a sense of her position.

This was a crisis in which she felt the positive necessity for prompt action, and her fertile mind conceived the plan of giving an entertainment to which she would invite the king, and by her fascinations woo him into reconciliation, and then to compliance with the appeal in behalf of her people.

With her womanly intuitions she had perceived
the assailable points in the king's character; she
knew his susceptibility to beauty, and determined
to adorn herself with all the appliances of the most
approved toilet, and to call to aid every artificial
lustre available to enhance her native charms: as
her case was urgent, policy was wise and diplomacy
excusable.

To appear before the king without an order or
invitation was an unprecedented liberty, and might
bring disgrace and consequent punishment upon
her, but she had made her resolution, and would
abide by it. Her fastidious taste suggested the
most effective arrangement of the various gifts
which her royal lord had bestowed upon her in his
happiness—the diamond rings, bracelets, and neck-
lace, all, she fitted conspicuously. This would, she
thought, flatter the king, and remind him of their
tender relations.

The crown which she took care to place on her
head was significant of her rights, and was a badge
of equality, through which she might demand and
expect acquiescence and favor.

As she stood at last before her mirror, contemplating in her beauty the might that would possibly set her people free from a terrible impending fate, the blent beauties of heaven seemed to aid her, and baptize her with almost divine beauty.

She hesitated until the last moment, when, throwing her head back, with eyes raised and hands stretched forward, she drank in an inspiration of heavenly hope, then stepped gracefully and confidently forward to where her lord was, in his audience-chamber.

He was carelessly regarding his courtiers, who were scattered around, when the sudden appearance of Esther seemed to startle the atmosphere of the room, as if a star had suddenly dropped from the heavens and glorified the scene.

The king was astonished, and in a moment so delighted with the novelty of her act that when she gracefully knelt before him he hesitated not a moment to extend the sceptre, and bid her rise and prefer any request which she might please; and when she assured him that it was only to claim his presence at a grand banquet, as she found it im-

possible to enjoy herself without his society, his
vanity, his chivalry, and his love were all aroused,
and he most graciously consented.

The lords and nobles stood gazing in boundless
admiration and genuine respect upon the lovely
vision, and Haman was flattered beyond measure
when she, through private motives of policy, selected him from the rest, and invited him also to
attend.

The king's coldness vanished like a mist before
the morning's sun; her presence revived a flow of
sweetest emotions, and Esther was almost sure that
she might make her real motives known; but she
suppressed her impatience until things might be
still more auspicious.

Haman was delighted; he dressed himself in his
richest attire, boasted to his wife of the great
honors he was considered worthy to receive, and
repaired with the king to Esther's banquet. She
suppressed the great indignation that she felt, and
entertained him becomingly. Haman had elegant
manners, for he was well cultivated in all court
etiquette, and was an accomplished lord of the

times; and he, no doubt, made himself amiable and graceful for the occasion; but Esther knew of the viper that lay concealed beneath this fair exterior, and loathed his presence in her heart.

But when the banquet was over and Haman went out, the gallows which he had had erected for Mordecai rose conspicuously and portentously against the sky, and brought back the hatred which Esther's sweetness and clemency had dispelled; he exulted in the thought that on the morrow his hated adversary would be hanging from that very gallows, and that before the closing morrow's sun there would not be left one of the despised race.

But wiser and higher influences were at work, influences which come unseen yet all-powerful, to frustrate evil designs and wicked machinations against the innocent.

It happened that the king could not sleep, though sweet, soft, gentle music stirred in the adjoining rooms, the dreamy moonlight streamed through the casement, and the very luxuriance of his couch suggested to the senses a lull, a soothing spell, an inducement to sleep; yet the king's thoughts went roving, his eyes were wide opened, and memory seemed to have set afloat old forgotten things, which arrayed themselves into speaking reminders; and at last one call upon his revived recollection caught and claimed attention.

Touching his summoning bell, his attendants came, of whom he requested that the archives of his kingdom should be brought; and, in the midst of his royal bed, he read an account which had vaguely suggested itself to his roving thoughts; that Mordecai, a Jew, had saved his life by disclosing a conspiracy, and that he had never been compensated or requited.

This struck the grateful vein of his feeling, and he determined to set about righting it.

It could have been no mere chance which dictated the opening of the book of records; it was a high power which instigated the act.

The stars had paled out before the morning sun, when Haman, hasting early to the palace to obtain audience with the king, for the purpose of having Mordecai instantly hung, passed Mordecai sitting as usual in the gate; the insignia of his race still

marked out, in soot, sackcloth, and ashes; yet still
as proud and silent, he gave no sign of humility or
respect. Haman arrived at the palace just in time
to receive the king's summons to appear at once in
the audience-chamber.

The king was glad, always, to have an adviser,
upon whom he might sometimes shift the weighty
affairs of state questions, and Haman was the man
whom he now needed to advise him what high
honors he should confer upon one who had done
great service to the king, and whom the king greatly delighted to honor.

Ever presumptuous in his estimate of his own
worth, he immediately conceived the opinion that
more startling honors were to be conferred upon
himself. He was certain that Haman was the object of royal clemency and favor; and when Ahasuerus, looking at him, satisfied that his answer
would relieve him of the burden of thinking of or
devising some scheme of great benefit, asked:
"What shall be done to the man whom the king
delighteth to honor?" he answered: "To the man
whom the king delighteth to honor let the royal

7

apparel be brought which the king useth to wear,
and the horse that the king rideth upon, and the
royal crown which is set upon his head, and let
this apparel and horse be delivered to the hands of
one of the king's most noble princes, that they may
array the man withal whom the king delighteth to
honor, and bring him on horseback through the
streets of the city, and proclaim before him : Thus
shall it be done to the man whom the king delighteth to honor."

This was a bold stroke, for the very insignia of
royalty were demanded, and these, doubtless, were
suggested to Haman on the ground that there was a
possibility that, through some unforeseen event, the
king's dominion might cease, and that he might be
exalted in his stead.

What terrible revulsion must have racked the
brain of Haman ; have torn his breast and dried his
tongue ; what blame did he not heap on his own
head for the infatuation which had dictated his
vanity ; what volcanoes of contending passion
rocked the foundations of his feeling, when the
king's answer declared that instead of himself these

THE MAN WHOM THE KING DELIGHTED TO HONOR.

honors were to go, all of them, to Mordecai, and at
his own instigation.

The king said: "Make haste, take the apparel
and the horse, as thou hast said, and do even so to
Mordecai, the Jew, who sitteth at the king's gate;
let nothing fail that thou hast spoken."

Of course Haman knew better than to remonstrate, for the laws of the Medes and Persians
were irrevocable. He bowed, and turned to obey.
He gave the message to Mordecai; was sullen and
calm, as he, with his own hands, acted chamberlain,
and arrayed him in robes of royalty and honor.

It really requires no very powerful stretch of the
imagination to describe a picture so striking as
these two men, so opposite in every point and particular, who now stood in the most peculiar positions one toward the other. Haman, dark-browed,
with the whole soul of suppressed hatred, defiance,
smothered wrath, and malignity, limned in his broad
profile; Mordecai receiving the honors as if entitled
to them, and seeming to show, by acceptance of his
services, that he was conferring and not receiving
honor.

The reason for the sudden and great favor must have puzzled Mordecai to analyze, yet he expressed no more surprise through his countenance than if it had been of every-day occurrence.

It did puzzle him; for when the pageant was concluded and the robes taken off and put away, he again occupied the same seat, and resumed the sackcloth and ashes; and his case did not seem changed, so far as externals were concerned or gave evidence. He had not heard from Esther, and the gallows prepared for him still stood, a monument of wrath against him, and he might, by the next night, be dangling from it a lifeless corpse.

It took all the faith of his sublime nature to enable him to adopt, in this hour, his own prophecy, that God would save his people, and through Esther.

Haman, in his shame and despair, went to his wife, and on woman's faithful bosom sobbed out a recitation of his woes. She, a seeress, foresaw the ruin of her house, told him that his day was over, and advised him to flee from the place in order to save his life, or take some prompt measure for his personal safety; but, while they were yet talking,

the king's chamberlain came, and hurried Haman
to Esther's banquet.

On the second day, at the banquet, the king
desired Esther to make *any* request of him, and it
should be granted, to the half of his kingdom. The
repentant king, doubtless, was anxious to reinstate
himself fully in the queen's affections, and wished
to prove it by some mark of especial favor, a love-
token.

The sublime character of Esther shows in strong
lines at this period. She might have demanded
that any sum or portion of riches should be settled
upon herself, and been sure of its being done in a
magnificent manner; but all and every thought of
personal favors were discarded and ignored, in her
self-sacrificing principle of devotion to those who
were a race persecuted, insulted, and suffering. If
the objects had been of *any* nation, class, or people
who were suspended under such a cruel penalty, her
pity would still have suggested the plea for their
lives; her motive was not merely her relation to
the Jewish race, but her philanthropic spirit was
her prompter.

Lovely, womanly, and beautiful, Esther appeared, as, gracefully kneeling her supple figure before her husband and king, she humbly, yet confidently and trustfully, raised her large, soft, gazelle-like eyes to his face, and, with the pathos of deep emotion controlling her musical voice, she uttered the simple words: "If I have found favor in thy sight, O king, and if it please the king, let my life be given at my petition, and my people at my request, for we are sold, I and my people, to be destroyed, to be slain, to perish." Then she disclosed her nationality and relationship to Mordecai, and quoted the edict which Haman had issued in the king's name, with his own signature and seal, and added: "But if we had been sold for bond-men and bond-women I had held my peace, although the enemy could not countervail the king's damage."

Such an appeal, uttered with all the fervor of enthusiasm, melted the king into the most profound emotion, and he inquired: "Who is he? Where is he that hath presumed in his heart to do so?"

Haman, confounded, speechless, dumb with consternation, inwardly craved of the gods to extin-

guish him on the spot sooner than allow him to be
made the scorn of the king and the rest; but wickedness meets its reward, and he had to face the position, and bear the levelling of eyes when Esther's
finger pointed out distinctly his figure amongst the
others, and she said the words: " *That* adversary,
THAT wicked man, is Haman."

The king, beyond himself with indignation and
rage at the weakness which he had suffered to
master him, the weakness of indolently allowing
himself to lean continually on another for advice
which his own kingly mind should have dictated—
especially as that confidant was now proven before
his face to be an arch deceiver, presumptuous,
crafty, and selfish—would not suffer his voice to give
any expression to his conflicting feelings, but went
out into the garden, possibly to take a moment in
which to consider his own premises, and line of pro-
cedure.

Esther, overcome by her temerity, and nearly
fainting from excess of emotion, threw her faultless
figure on a couch, rested her head upon one hand,
whilst her fairy little feet peeped out from the edge

of her royal robe. She was the very impersonation of beauty, the realization of the most enthusiastic Persian's ideal of perfection.

Haman, crucified by horror at his prospects of disgrace, banishment, or probably ignominious death, realized that the queen's prayers alone could save him; and in his extremity forgot all else and threw himself beside her, imploring her to sue for him.

At this unfortunate moment, the king entered, and, seeing Haman in that position, white with rage and just indignation, he exclaimed: "What, will he violate the queen here in my own palace!"

This was sufficient. Haman's face was covered—significant token; the attendants took him out, and the hangman hung him upon the gallows which he had had erected for Mordecai, and which was fifty cubits high. Thus perished a man whose wickedness suggested the destruction of a nation, from motives of personal jealousy.

Esther's humane nature could not rejoice in the sufferings of any one, but in this act she realized that her nation was saved from the cruel edict.

Ahasuerus could not unsay what he had once said, for the Persian law was irrevocable, but he gave the Jews each one the privilege of defending himself, and in this way they came out victorious, and Esther's affectionate heart reverenced the king, and loved, most fondly, her husband.

After that every day recorded some boon which the king granted her. Mordecai was made prime minister, and the Hebrews were all well provided for.

To the disposition of Esther, to her noble character, and to her piety, we call especial attention. When, suddenly reduced to poverty, exiled and dependent on her own delicate hands for every service, she retained her patience, took up the lines of life as they had fallen to her, and worked them up into a beautiful fabric of cheerful adaptation.

Upon her exaltation to the throne, the quick shifting of the scenes in the drama of her life did not disturb the equable exercise of every amiable trait, but brought out into more perfect light through contrast the noblest purposes and strength of intellect, the severest virtue, the strictest probity, the

7*

most unqualified devotion, the most enthusiastic patriotism, and the most startling comparisons of moral will with baleful influences.

Throughout every vicissitude of trial and triumph she had held to her unflinching faith in God, and had unhesitatingly obeyed, with child-like simplicity, her adopted father Mordecai; had held to the principles which her early education indoctrinated, and never for a moment lost the true sense of her obligation to her fellow-creatures. Sacred to all hearts be the memory of Esther, the Star!

Now as a star still brighter she presides,
Where one continuous joy abides.
True virtue's royalty crowns her head;
By majesty of good her life is led.
The beautiful deed has won its meed,
And flowers of faith have riped their seed.
The stars that decked her earthly name
Shine brighter now mid heavenly fame.

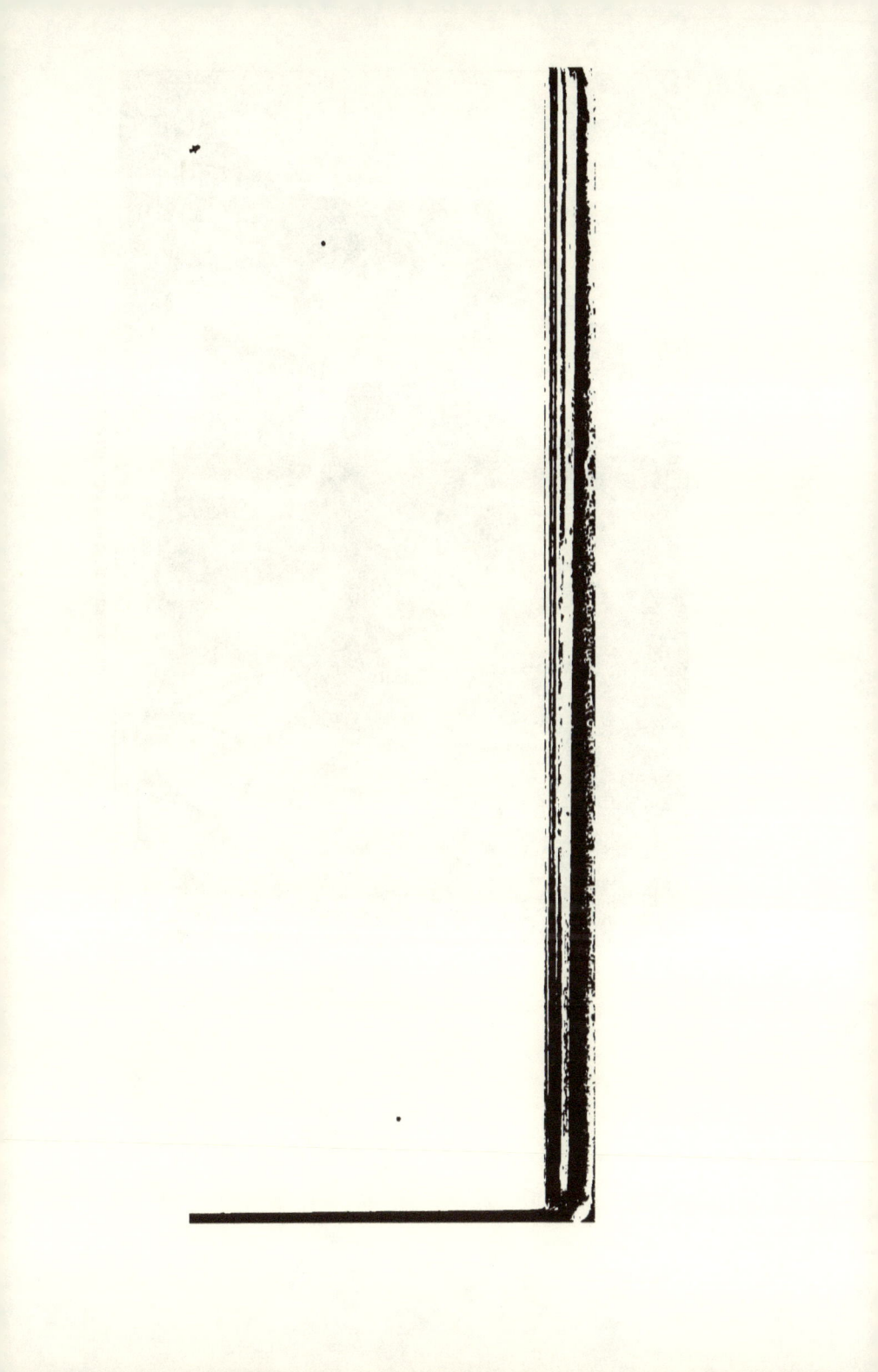

THE EMERALD AND MARY BEFORE CHRIST.

IV.

The Emerald.

MARTHA.

"She riseth also while it is yet night, and giveth meat to her household, and a portion to her handmaids."

MANY had been the changes in the East between the time that Ruth gleaned in the fields, that Adah was sacrificed, and the day that Martha entertained beneath her own roof "Jesus the Messiah."

Wars and rumors of war had shook the earth and sent alarms; famine had desolated the land; pestilence depopulated whole sections of a once-happy country. Political factions had grown up; policy had levelled cliques; monarchs had been dethroned, and demagogues been exalted.

Drought and flood, fire and chance, had brought their usual degrees of disparity; yet the sun shone as brightly, the stars twinkled as gleefully, the moon was as tender, and the earth as willing as ever.

Men and women married and were given in marriage, and humanity had the same law of feeling. The gold of Ophir, the ships of Tarsus, the dyes from Tyre, and the fine linen from Sidon, were still in vogue.

The whole Jewish nation, though separated by many leagues of land and water, was existent, and still clung tenaciously to the law of Moses, and served in the tabernacle.

The Mediterranean was still pictured with the tremulous lily. The blood-red rose blossomed amidst the skulls of the battle-field. Diamond and gold mines hoarded treasures, which men still made ambitious plans to secure.

Trade and commerce existed; men were subject to the same passions; no law in nature was affected, and yet the epoch of Christ's birth had come, the system of atonement been instituted.

When we think of the preaching of the Apostles, their declaration that the Lord God Almighty had come down from Heaven, and dwelt as mortal man among the people, we are surprised that such a scheme had not changed the whole aspect of the world; that all men were not converted to angels; and that trade and merchandise were necessary to sustain human interests; we wonder that tares ever grew again in the soil of earth.

The Jews never realized that their Redeemer existed in the poor Nazarene. Their Messiah, that Isaiah sang about, was to be clothed with pomp and majesty; his crown was to outshine all other diadems. His sceptre should be potent to elevate the whole race to dignity and honor, and to restore Jerusalem to its pristine grandeur.

Only a few of the Jews recognized Jesus of Nazareth as the Mediator.

Not far from Jerusalem, in the town of Bethany, there was one little Jewish family who became converts to Christ's doctrine, though they did not

really understand the full significance of his mission. They regarded him in the light of a friend,
and truly and sincerely were they attached to him.

Of the virtue and moral beauty of the characters
in this little family, every school-child has been
taught. The circumstance of the death and restora-
tion of Lazarus is a household story.

The actual history of any of the New Testament
characters is so bare, has so limited a margin for
speculation, that but little room is found for traditional embellishment.

Many efforts have been made to afford detail,
with such poor success, that we determine to take
the original tersely-rendered story of Martha, and
give it, without embellishments of startling style, in
its most natural manner, to our readers.

So much merit blends in Martha's character, that
any varnish of high color or eulogy would set as
badly in a picture of her life as frippery and tinsel
would have been out of taste in her toilet.

The house owned and occupied by Martha, Mary,
and Lazarus, in the village of Bethany, was of
moderate dimensions. It was of ancient date, and

ivy clustered around its walls.   Cool and pleasant
the trees made the ground around, and the shadow
of Lebanon reached nearly to the spot.   The brook
Kedron swept its crystal flood not far distant, and
Olivet met the kisses of the sky all in full sight.

Plenty was pictured in the aspect of this retired
place, and from the doorway, throughout the
house, there was never to be seen speck nor stain to
offend the most fastidious.   Neatness was apparent.
There was no need to inquire if a tasteful and industrious woman presided over the premises,—the
assurance of it was observable in every object that
met the eye.

Martha, Mary, and Lazarus composed the family
proper.   Martha possessed, to an eminent degree,
administrative ability.   She was leader of the domestic *ménage*, a position which called into active
play her especial talents.

Her mother realized, before her death, that
Martha would be trustworthy as manager and head
of the family after she was gone, and felt no apprehensions of the proper training of the more delicate
and sensitive Mary.

Long before the dawn fretted the sky, Martha
was stirring; appointing the services peculiar to the
day, setting in motion the machinery of domestic
business, and arranging the maids at their tasks.
Theirs was a family of consequence in the village:
she had her servants.

Even those in moderate circumstances had hire-
lings and apprentices. We do not exaggerate when
we say that Martha arose so early, for it was the
custom of the people of the country. The most
delightful part of the twenty-four hours, in sultry cli-
mates, is before the sun rises. The air then seems
to be impregnated with an element which invigorates
the lax frame for the coming action of the sun's rays.

Repeated instances are mentioned in the Scrip-
tures of the system of early rising. Kings and
princes had the habit of rising before the dawn.
Moses was commanded to stand before Pharaoh
early in the morning as he came forth to the water.

Martha's habit of taking time by the forelock was
not altogether the result of custom, but was also
the natural sign of her industry, vigilance, economy,
and activity.

She loved to send her orisons forth upon the wings of morning, and she also believed that it would secure health for her sister, who was not, it seems, of so vigorous and energetic a constitution as herself.

Besides, Martha was thrifty, and looked well to the ways of her household. She chose, as all industrious housekeepers *will*, to secure a margin of daylight by husbanding the dawn; she never let noon trip up the heels of her morning duties.

Everybody knows how agreeable a' house may be in which a cheerful spirit of energy is cultivated by its mistress; one who takes hold of duty with joy, and keeps her actions springing upon the hinges of willingness.

The atmosphere of such a household reflects content, and visitors feel refreshed, as a traveller does who comes across a widespread tree when its branches are filled with sweet singing-birds. If the mistress be querulous and complaining, no one who comes under her influence perceives a green tree with musical songsters, but, instead, withering boughs, with croaking ravens upon them.

There was a sense of repose in Martha's house, a kind of rest, such as one experiences when suddenly rid of a deafening roar of water or machinery, or the pressure of a heavy burden upon the arm. It was physical rest as well as spiritual repose; there was in the atmosphere a quiet, mingled with the serenade murmuring of domestic machinery, which satisfied the mind that comforts for the body were in process of preparation.

The three orphans were not forgetful of their obligations to their Maker, but gave grateful response through their cheerful willingness to take life as it was presented. They realized, through every sense, the gratification intended; philosophically regarded the benefits of Providence, despising nothing, however trifling in value, that came in their way, through which the kindness of a wise Creator might be recognized. Martha, especially, applied to actions the injunction, "Whatsoever you do, do it heartily, as to the Lord, and not unto men."

These orphans were well thought of in Bethany, and were of consequence, for the town was called the "Town of Martha and Mary." They were Israelites, and practised all the Jewish customs in their family and household.

They became devoted disciples of Jesus; through his pious teachings perfected themselves, and lived more spiritedly up to the Mosaic commandments. To love their God with all their hearts was a privilege out of which grew their love for their neighbors.

Mary was the opposite to Martha in many traits of disposition. It is usual for us to find, among a family of five or six, great differences of character, intellect, and person. Martha was vivacious, energetic, nervous, and emphatic.

Positive in principle, she believed that religion could be applied in every hour of one's existence; was to be *lived*, and not merely *observed*; that it was something which might be practised in the occupation, design, and exigencies of every-day existence; circumscribed by, and subject to, no limited prescription of text and letter.

Martha exerted her piety through every avocation; she applied it as an instrument by which all

keynotes might be sounded, and believed it suit-
able to be played throughout every section of the
passing page of existence. She was firm in resolve,
lofty in aspiration, strong in effort, and invincible in
integrity.

 From Martha's industry there seemed to emanate
an inspiration for her handmaidens, each of whom
worked cheerfully, as if for pleasure, and not for
wages.

There was a halo of geniality which accompanied
her, and brightened the aspect of each department
in which she was engaged. This sprang from hope;
was the fulfillment of the lively faith that always
actuated her. To *believe* in the constant protection
of a superior Providence was her *principle*, the
burden of every act. Upon this parallel she
brought out every minor aspiration.

Martha was a lily raising its head high, and
claiming of heaven the dew that it promised.
Mary, the violet which hung its head, fearing that
the dew might not deem it of sufficient worth to
baptize; shrinking and timid, yet lovely and tender,
waiting to be taught, never claiming to teach.

Martha, as we have said, was more vigorous than Mary in constitution, and in person was opposite. Her hair, naturally rich in curls, she, in her severe ideas of simplicity, combed back straight from her brow.   Her eyes were large and sparkling, her mouth firm yet very tender.

She was beyond average height, and properly proportioned. Mary was small of stature, fair and more *spirituelle* in appearance ; her hair was of unusual length and beauty.   Never had it been, she thought, so highly adorned as when spangled with crystal drops that adhered when she made of it a napkin for her Saviour's feet.

Martha's position, as mistress of a family, had matured her manners into a matronly dignity, which enhanced the charm of her temperamental vivacity, and secured a serenity of movement which was well matched with her person. She possessed eminently the great charm of woman, repose of manner ; from this no sudden transition of feeling could throw her.

Any peculiar emotion was manifested by heightened color, the paling or brightening of her eye, and

the dilation of her nostril. Enthusiasm portrayed
its zeal in her speaking countenance, not through
any abrupt movement of her person. Joy could
tune her voice and play with it varied intonations,
but could not tempt her into any boisterous manifestation. "Martha was troubled about many
things," the Scripture says.

To be the responsible mistress of a family is no
light position to hold, especially when one has so
dear a charge as an only sister and brother to make
comfortable and happy. She was vitally spiritual,
though she gave less time to rituals than did her
sister.

Prayer is in its highest sense the aspiration of
the heart, and can be achieved while the body and
hands are vigorously exercised. It does not require
the position of kneeling to effect its utterance. It
is a force which finds articulation at the right
moment, and is limited by no terms of contortion.
Martha cultivated it in every season, however com-
plicated and vexed, of her life.

Besides the usual complement of domestic labor,
she had her garden of beautiful sweet shrubs and

luxuriant vegetables to superintend; azalias, roses, pomegranates, and jessamines mixed their sweets together and flourished under her thrifty hand.

Every one who had ground raised grapes and made their own wine. Martha's clusters of purple, which in those latitudes grow to fabulous size, doubtlessly fulfilled the very highest promise of cultivation. She had goats which must be milked, and in her dairy were to be found sweet butter and young cheese.

Her vines were her tender inspirers; she realized that no object of nature affords so great a variety of allusions as the vine: the widespreading boughs, broad leaves, and clustering bunches of luscious look and glad taste, continually suggested symbols to her mind.

The faithful Thomas, the companion of Christ, the *confidante* and friend of Lazarus, figured in these pictures; sweet thoughts of love engrossed her as she coupled him in her mind with a fruitful bough whose branches might even at some future time overshadow herself.

She made wine for the good of her family, and
8

with her own hand manufactured linen-cloth; she
also embroidered her brother's girdles.

She was, of necessity, compelled to be careful
about many things, and worked willingly, or "with
the delight of her hands." Throughout her whole
life there was a firmness and consistency of character shown which is worthy of the highest admiration.

This, in woman's character, is a virtue demand-
ing great exercise of moral and religious principle;
because affection and feeling unavoidably influence
women generally, which renders them unstable in
opinion and liable to changes of temperament and
disposition.

Mary's relation to Martha seemed more like that
of daughter to mother, from the fact of the difference in their dispositions, though in reality there
was but a small disparity in their years.

Mary's acute sensibility and devotional mind
readily imbibed a fervor of religious strictness, so
that sacrament and sacrifice were associated with
every idea of duty, and disposed her to a rigid observance of sacred forms; made her more poetical

and less practical than exactly accorded with Martha's positive ideas.

Martha believed that ordinance, combined with the appliances of labor, was more apt to effect *rapport* with the spirit of Omnipotence than the total neglect of utility for sacrament.

Mary, doubtlessly, was very lovely in disposition and manner, as well as in her person. She had soft eyes, as tender as a dove's; her lips could not be painted and justice be done them. Over her whole countenance was diffused an angelic expression. Loving, quiet, gentle, devoted, she would have made the most ardent nun, for she was never so well pleased as when engaged in performing the strict duties of the sanctuary.

Martha sometimes thought that her zeal was carried to excess, and attempted to reason with her upon the necessity of attendance to the actual requirements of material life. At such times, Mary would meekly contemplate her sister, promise to fulfill her injunctions; but, in the midst of her task, would evince so much repugnance for them, that Martha was fain to leave her to her own way.

On one occasion, when the duties of housekeeping had accumulated, and Martha's busy hands and fertile brain were not sufficient to conceive and perform, she sadly complained to Jesus of Mary's indifference to her heavy responsibilities.

She was mortified and pained at the rebuke contained in His answer: "Martha, Martha, thou art troubled about many things, but Mary has chosen the better part, which shall not be taken from her."

Martha sorrowfully turned and left Mary sitting at His feet, drinking in the beautiful language of inspiration that fell from his lips; she contrasted the pleasure which she might take in His teaching, with the positive necessity that existed of her carefully providing comfortable cheer for the beloved Guest, but, with her usual self-sacrificing spirit, accepted the blame, determining to perform double part and let Mary have the full benefit of His society, since *she* was debarred from the privilege; practical in everything, in self-sacrifice and mortification, as well as in performance of physical labor.

When the snow-white cloth was laid, which was the work of her own hands, Martha remembered

that while the shuttle was flying back and forth
through the web, she had lifted up her heart to her
God and begged him to weave her every action into
a woof of perfect good.

When the sweet butter was brought, she thought
of the prayer her soul had uttered as she churned
it; to implore God to create in the depths of her
heart, all good resolves, and enable her to turn them
out in accomplishment of effort.

When the ripe fruit was placed in the baskets,
she called to mind her wishes while gathering it,
that she might be ripened or developed into full
fruition of wisdom and goodness. She was comforted when she reflected that, through her inde-
fatigable industry, her beloved Jesus would be com-
fortably fed and entertained.

About Bethany there were many pleasant ram-
bles, and in the twilight of evening the sisters often
went out to meet Lazarus when he was returning
home from his business. Once, they were delighted
at the unexpected sight of Jesus and Thomas in
company with him. Thomas was the dear friend and
confidant of Lazarus, and also a disciple of Christ.

The brook sang its measures; the stars shone; the sweet summer-breezes rustled through the scarlet cactus-blossoms; Martha's heart throbbed to the sweet emotions of love, for Thomas held her hand, and the Christ, the Prince of Peace, walked beside them.

Wondrous privilege had they; and yet they humanly regarded him as was best and right.

Had they realized that God was in Jesus they could not have held him in the sweet estimation of friend. Their awe for so august a presence would have made wide separation between them. Mary's sweet eyes beamed with a holy fire. While she listens to his teachings, her heart beats responsive: her feet touched the sward lightly in time to her joy, and her voice assumed its most melodious tones.

Martha looked strangely beautiful and queen-like, as she walked by the one she loved with human love.

Ah! love *will exist*, even though the feet of Jesus tread beside; naught that ever yet touched the soul has power to hush the strain which was instituted in Paradise. Martha's face shone with its reflection, the whole atmosphere took its likeness from the glad inspirer, emotion was set to pulse, which strung the harp of her soul, and played on it the sweetest melodies that ever made glad her heart.

The murmurs of Kedron sounded like whispering voices of angels.

To Jesus, who heard all the still tones of nature, who communed continually with the invisible agents, the very breeze that fanned his cheek was vocal with the messages and love-tokens of his celestial inspirers. Nothing was a mystery to him; he read prophecy in everything, from the dream of his sleep to the death of a friend.

His soul was open to spirit sight; he kept company with prophets, priests, martyrs, and kings, through his gift.

By him the sky was fathomed, space defined, and sublimity comprehended. He saw the course of a soul when freed from its tabernacle of clay, and followed the flight of mind from one stage to another of immortal progression.

On this particular evening his tongue burned with eloquence, his speech suited the understanding of his friends. Mary and Lazarus walked on beside him, Martha and Thomas behind. Sweet flowers grew on the borders of their path; the glowworm gave light to the dewdrop which bathed the violet. Summer exulted in fragrance and mellow tints.

Meantime, heaven watched, with its eyes of stars, upon the devoted head that walked that evening beneath its canopy.

When they reached the house, the white cluster-roses that gleamed through the mist of evening were heavy with fragrance, and Jesus took one that Mary gathered, the sweetest spray, and held it in his hand. His hands, soft and tender, although inured to toil, were fit and meet to handle flowers, things which bring a sense of peace and rest, and typify purity.

After they had gone into the house, Martha brought a vessel of water, and Mary bathed the feet of Jesus with her hands; this was a custom which Jews were careful to observe, and was most grateful to Jesus, who had wearily trodden the rough ground; the stones had bruised his feet, and it must have been a positive luxury to have his tired members manipulated by woman's tender hands.

Jesus loved this family tenderly and truly; he was *confidant*, friend, and counsellor to them, and their house was a retreat which he gladly availed himself of.

Without a roof for his head, or a couch for his body to lie on, persecuted, misunderstood, misappreciated, despised, and slandered, this home was to him a bright spot in his existence : the cordiality of their friendship touched his heart, as dew refreshes flowers. No amount of adulation bestowed upon a king could have brought so sweet a savor: their affection was bestowed upon a despised Nazarene, a poor carver of wood.

Their purity of motive could not be questioned. For through Jesus they saw no promise of future emolument, no incentive to a mode of policy. There was no governmental office in prospective for them to play for; no judicial post to aspire to, no rank, no gift to hope for; they loved Jesus of Nazareth, and he knew it, because of his goodness, his wisdom, his powerful gifts, and for his affection manifested toward them.

Not until long afterward did these three realize

8*

the significance of his name, the sublimity of his character. Still, Martha's faith was so unqualified, so clear, so full, that she believed him capable of performing any feat, however wonderful; there is nothing that he taught but was treasured in her thoughtful mind. And after the dear one was buried and had risen, these things came back before her, and she saw plainly what it all meant,—that the Comforter whom he promised to send them, after he was united to the Father, was the Spirit of himself.

Even when Jesus discoursed to them about the destruction of the temple, and its reorganization on the third day, it did not occur to them in its full significance.

Martha's generous management was never more cheerfully appropriated, than when this loved Guest tarried with them; cool linen, smelling of rose-leaves, she placed upon his bed, arranged flowers on his table, fixed a hundred other little appreciative appliances in his bedchamber, all of which were grateful to the refined tastes of Jesus.

The appointments of the whole establishment were

such as secured him sweet recreation after his buf-
fetings with rough men, who were deaf to his
teaching, inappreciative, and who even sought his
life.

Every one has, sometime or other, sat at a lux-
uriously furnished table, where form and fashion
prescribed the terms, and can contrast their sensa-
tions at that meal with those experienced at a
dinner that was served in a less costly manner, yet
where the host and hostess presided, and dispensed
fervent, unadulterated hospitality.

Offices of love, served by willing, ready hands,
were what was accepted and gladly appreciated by
the lonely Nazarene. He often spoke to Martha in
praise of her beautiful dishes and arrangement of
household affairs, which praise was worth to her
more than rubies and gold.

We know that the brain is dependent, very much,
upon the stomach, and that through the act of
digestion is the mind and disposition kept healthy
and amiable, or the reverse; that digestion is pro-
moted or retarded by the quality of food taken into
the stomach; to insure sufficient nutriment to the

---

blood, phosphorus to the brain, and albumen to the bones, this law of hygiene should be well understood by the director of the culinary department of a house. Martha succeeded in making her table-fare wholesome as well as agreeable. Everything that she undertook she performed thoroughly; her good sense, forethought, and discrimination were rarely led into mistake.

It was their *privilege* to have plenty; simplicity was their *rule*. Martha's lot was cast where vigilance and effort were imperative. She knew that if she faltered in the faithful discharge of her appointed duties, those dearest to her must consequently lose many of their indulgences.

Sometimes housewives in their zeal to have their respectability sustained, become indifferent to the interests which affect their eternal welfare; they forget the transitory nature of secular pursuits; how quickly what seems of most importance to the mortal may suddenly drop from their hands and perish, or that they may, in a moment's time, be separated from earth, from friends, wealth, rank, and influence, and be transferred to a sphere where the consequences of misapplied energies and talents will be regret and disappointment.

Jesus at one time perceived that Martha might possibly become too much absorbed in worldly matters, and hence his timely rebuke. "Martha, Martha, thou art troubled about many things. Mary has chosen the better part, which shall not be taken from her."

Lazarus had the management of their joint patrimony, and was successful and prosperous in his business.

He was a young man of middle stature, athletic, and healthy; he had the complexion and expression of Mary. He was refined, his temperament poetical, and his tendencies religious. He had great taste for beauty, and a keen appreciation of power of intellect; was a comfort in every respect to his sisters. His habits had always been above reproach. He engaged in none of the boisterous games of the age, nor followed any vice; was very beautiful in features, and was a fit mate for his beloved friend Thomas.

The fact that Jesus chose Lazarus for an intimate

companion, justifies us in ascribing to him the very
highest moral, mental, and spiritual attributes.
Their friendship was faster than that of brothers,
and they rejoiced together over all that was
presented to them through the divine sight of
Jesus.

Great indeed was the spiritual benefit conferred
upon the little family by the companionship of
Jesus; we may conceive that hosts of angels
attended Christ, that a train and retinue of unseen,
invisible spirits, gathered around, and encompassed
him in their charmed circle, shielding, guarding, and
ministering to him. The whole house must have
been overshadowed by their influence, whenever
Jesus rested in it.

The prophecies of Martha's favorites, David and
Isaiah, occurred to her: "The angels of the Lord
encampeth around about them that fear him ;" and
again: "I will give my angels charge concerning
thee, that they bear thee up in their hands, lest at
any time thou dash thy foot against a stone." And
yet more: "The angels shall minister to him."

Oh! what privilege had Martha; to have a guest

who kept company with angels; who saw heaven open, and who was conversant with Moses and the Prophets!

But Jesus was very much persecuted by the people, so much so that it was not safe for him to stay about Jerusalem; so with many tears and lamentations the family of Bethany assented, at the last moment, to the scheme of his retirement to another section.

They went with him a part of the way, and tried to lighten the journey by every means they could devise. Martha prepared nice bread and cake, and put up a bottle of her own wine for him to refresh himself with. Mary worked his girdle and placed within it a testimonial of her love and tender interest. When at last they had to separate, they kissed him and returned.

Many were their apprehensions concerning him, until they heard that he had reached Bethabara, and that he had some of his disciples with him.

Martha, after his departure, prophetically conjectured that some calamity would happen to them, and could not stifle her apprehensions. With these forebodings she did not care to distress Mary, who was already afflicted at the departure of Jesus. Martha was prepared for the illness of Lazarus, which commenced soon after, and which terminated so fatally.

The dearly-beloved, affectionate, beautiful brother was stricken down with a nervous disorder, and despite the skill of the Jewish doctors, who were very attentive and learned besides, and the unceasing ministrations of the two afflicted sisters, he grew worse and worse. At this point Martha wrote to Jesus, and sent the letter by an especial messenger, informing him of the illness of Lazarus.

This one act is sufficient to demonstrate the indomitable faith of Martha; the fact of the wording of the letter. She used no entreaties, put forth no complaints, uttered no murmurs, but only said : " Our brother Lazarus, whom you love, is sick nigh unto death." She believed that the knowledge of their need would be sufficient to bring Jesus straight to them ; she knew of his wonderful powers to heal, and felt sure that all would be well if he could once more return.

Wonderful faith is this, which realizes that the demand of the soul will be sufficient to insure its supply.

Of course, it was not necessary for Jesus to receive written intimation of the illness of his friend, for his soul perceived his condition, though leagues of land and water separated them.   Yet he went not, at once, for he knew that there was a particular purpose to effect, and he remained away intentionally.

In the meantime Lazarus, young, fresh, vigorous, and the beloved of Jesus, withered and wasted, his pulse sank, and at last, without a groan or sign of pain, he took on the deep sleep from which the doctors and friends never expected to see him restored.

Great was the agony of distress into which the sisters were thrown, though Martha still expected Jesus, and believed that he could give them consolation.   All families of consequence about Jerusalem had vaults; Martha had a family-tomb where were laid her father and mother; into this was Lazarus laid away, after they had kept him out three days.

Martha wandered about restlessly. It was the custom with the Jews for the doctors to stay with the family after the decease of their patient, and to render all the comfort in their power; the house is also put in mourning, and the bereaved are draped in the sable symbols of woe. Martha could not sit still; a spirit of restlessness occupied her. On the fourth day after her brother's death, she perceived that Jesus was near, and ran to meet him.

She fell upon her knees and uttered the words: "If thou hadst been here my brother had not died;" and after his answer, added: "but I know that even now, whatsoever thou wilt ask of the Father he will give it thee." Wondrous faith! her heart throbbed with expectancy; her Lord had come, and she trusted him.

Thomas, at the first intimation of Lazarus' death, had, while the other apostles urged him not to go where so short a time before the Jews had tried to stone him, begged Jesus to accompany him back, for his grief was so great that he said, "Let us go back, and *die* with him."

He was now in company with Jesus, and the tears

of Martha greatly distressed and pained him. He
looked wistfully at the friend of whom so much was
always expected, and when Martha retired to call
Mary and give her secret information of the arrival
of the beloved Jesus, Thomas moved involuntarily
toward the sepulchre, having hold of the arm of
Jesus; then Mary came forward and related her
woes. "Jesus wept."

The history of the tragedy at the sepulchre all
are so familiar with, that we cannot invest the simple fact with any description which would seem new
or add interest. It speaks for itself, and the great
nature of the event is beyond mere rhythmetrical
calculation to portray. But the strength of Martha's character shone out through the trying
ordeal; serene and calm she stood, while the voice
of her Lord called aloud for Lazarus to come
forth.

There were many present who did not believe
that Christ could effect the end he proposed; even
Mary trembled with apprehension. What if he
failed? his own reputation was at stake as well as
her hope; the Jews stood ready to accuse him of

making false professions if he failed, and equally ready to accuse and condemn him if he succeeded. Thomas stood by holding a hand of each of the sisters; his heart beating quick, his sympathies keenly alive, his anxiety intense.

It was indeed a moment of *great suspense.* Stout hearts and strong faith were necessary for the occasion. The servants stood grouped around the two sisters, contemplating them with serious eyes; those who had been accustomed to regard Martha as a person of superior mind and fortitude, watched her with suspended breath; they perceived that she was equal to the crisis; the faith that had prompted her speech—"Even now, if thou wilt ask the Father, he will give thee Lazarus back to life," sustained her. She believed, and she realized.

After Lazarus was restored, and his energies somewhat resuscitated, he was lifted in solicitous hands to his house. Mary sat at his feet and bathed them with glad tears, while Martha, radiant with the lustre of hope realized, daintily fed him with nourishing food; Thomas knelt beside her, while Jesus, the wonderful Physician, stood contemplating the result of his skill, the observed of all observers. Martha's cheeks were deeply dyed with scarlet, always a sign with her of great emotion ; her hand trembled a little, while her eyes beamed with a hundred new joys.

Lazarus was so contented, so easy, so sweetly compelled to be administered to, that his senses, still weak from long fasting and confinement in the vault, were scarcely yet able to realize that he was not in a state of beatitude.

There were enemies on the scene, fierce scowlers, who were even *then* concocting plans to murder this great Healer, and who soon went out to take counsel together for his destruction.

After a few days the household of this "little family" was restored to its usual order, and Martha assiduously applied herself, with renewed dispatch, to her domestic duties.

She left Mary to attend personally to Lazarus, who was somewhat weak and unsettled, whilst she traversed every department. Like humming-birds, her feet flew about with the alacrity of affection and interest ; every one of her movements was dictated by thankfulness; for Lazarus, her beloved brother, was among them again, brought up from the grave; for HIM now she might work; her old incentive was restored.

Thomas, also, the inspirer of all sweet melodies of her heart, her pattern of excellence and picture of beauty, was near her.

Martha was so great in her excellence of faith, that she worked as but few ever did. She *lived* and *practised* her faith, through every moment of secular life; well might Thomas regard her as a miracle of beauty, amiability, and Christian virtue.

This friend, counsellor, physician, was compelled to secrete himself. Thomas, John, and Martha privately arranged a mode of administering to him, as long as it might be necessary for him to remain secreted.

It was late one evening, when the shadows had grown thick, the dew was falling, and the murmurs of Salem came through the distance, that a group of four or five might have been found standing under the shades of a Lebanon cedar. Sobs, incapable of repression, smote the still atmosphere. Mary was leaning her head upon the bosom of Jesus, taking leave of her beloved Lord; amid so many threatening dangers, she believed that she would not meet him again. He kissed her, spoke consoling words, and was gone out into the darkness, while Mary and another sorrowfully went home again.

Joyful was the effect of His appearance again, when, six days before the Passover, he came straight to the house of his friends. Many strangers were anxious to behold him who was capable of such wondrous deeds.

And Martha, ever watchful of his dignity, proud for his honor, proposed to her brother and sister that they give him a great feast or supper. A supper under such circumstances, she knew, would prove their appreciation of him to the whole people; for among the Jews a manifestation of that kind was an *especial* honor to the one to whom it was given. A supper denoted full fellowship and perfect friendship.

To this both agreed; so with joyful alacrity they set about to have prepared all that culinary skill could devise for the table, or that good taste and

---

ingenuity might suggest for the full pleasure of the occasion.

It was a success. The most remarkable act of Martha, but one which was entirely characteristic of her perfection of Christian character, was her humility in serving with her own hands at the table.

Her elastic figure swayed gracefully back and forth in her polite service. She wore a flowing robe of green, with a soft, white lace-veil which shaded her beautiful throat, and was lightly thrown back from her pure brow. One single ornament she wore—a sprig of green, a bit of cedar which Thomas had begged her to wear, reminding her that it was a fit emblem of her faith and constancy to all whom she claimed as friends.

Thomas gallantly assisted her to serve, or to wait upon the table, and we may imagine what an impression her act of humility before this large company created, for she was a woman of rank, and in circumstances above any such office. They ascribed consequence to a guest who was worthy of such an act of devoted attention.

Joyfully fled the hours to the guests generally,

though to some there was a sorrowful beckoning of
calamity, and Jesus himself knew of what cup he
must soon drink.

We must leave Martha while the hour is rosy
with hope and joy; while the beautiful inspiration of
faith lighted her eyes, and gave swift step to her
feet; while the pleasure of sight was hers, and the
realization of the presence of those dearest on earth
to her, made glad her heart; while Jesus was there,
and light and music and wine painted red the season.

We *must* draw the curtain before the darkness
which settled upon Gethsemane is presented; before the vail of the Temple is rent in twain.

Nothing that could be woven farther would constitute a more perfect picture than what we have
already tried to portray; of Martha's faith, industry, zeal, truth, and constancy, manifested not only
through outward observance in sanctified places,
but in every action and event of her private life.

Martha stands prominent and fairest in the galaxy
of "Faithful Ones;" may each and all of her sisters,
in Israel and in Christendom, imitate her excellent
example.

9

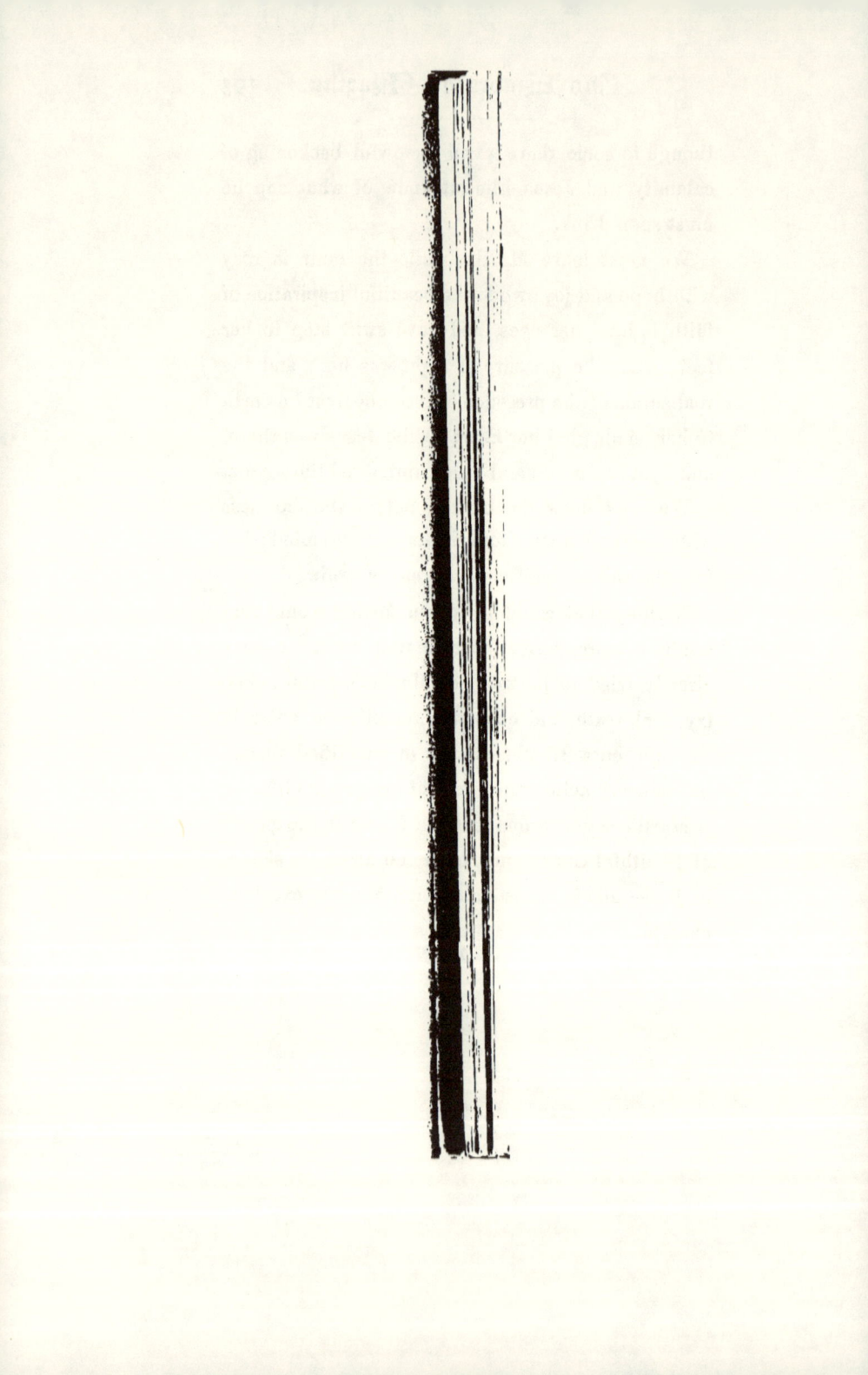

THE RUBY, AN ASSEMBLY OF THE FOLLOWERS OF CHRIST.

V.

The Ruby.

ELECTA.

T was midnight. In an elegant room, upon a luxurious couch, a matron slept. The moonbeams came in at the window; not being satisfied to burnish into splendor the silver mountings of the furniture, they stole across the Persian carpet, and kissed the hair, eyes, and lips of the beautiful lady; and invisible angels were there, "encamping about her whom the Lord loved."

Worthy was she of the ministration of angels, for she was full of grace, moral virtue, and practical piety. While the moonbeams ravished her face, she was dreaming; the pictures painted upon her

sleep were doubtlessly intended for prophetic warnings.

She dreamt that it was a future day, full of
turbulence; that strange factions had sprung up,
for which men and women were willing to be martyrs; she saw bloodshed, a mob, a rough giant, who
came forward and proposed terms, which he said
would be sufficient to expiate some gross offence
she had committed, but what, she did not perceive;
she declined his terms; he gave her blows, dragged
her by the hair, and she was about to perish when
she saw a light, and from it came a voice, saying:
"Whosoever believeth in me, though he perish, yet
will I sustain him."

The dawn of morning broke over the world, the
sunshine replaced the moonbeams, light of day
baptized her face, compelled the ugly vision to pass,
and restored the cheerful consciousness of safety
which morning always brings; but for a long time
the impression of Electa's dream remained fixed
upon her mind, and thrills of apprehension would
seize her when she related it.

The dwelling of Electa was of a style of archi-

tecture which the extravagant period of her grand-
parents recommended; gold and silver were not
rare in panellings, cornice, and doors. Built of the
finest material that artisans could find, and embel-
lished without regard to cost, it stood, fair and
elegant to behold from the exterior, pleasant, cheerful, and splendid within. A fit abode was this for
our " Chosen Lady."

Electa had been brought up amidst the gorgeous
scenes and circumstances of Oriental wealth, and
when she inherited this residence and came to oc-
cupy it, she delighted to add improvements, and to
adorn it with some of the fashions of her far-distant
native East. Luxury abounded, yet good taste and
reason controlled the appointments of this extensive
establishment.

The situation was one of exceeding beauty; romantic and picturesque, it yet retained enough of
what we call feudal aspect to inspire us with an
idea of the chivalric days when heroes assembled
with their legions at the feast, where the victor, pre-
ferring honor to conquest, might be imagined riding
up to the very door to have the badge of victory,

made of holly-leaves, placed upon his brow by the ruler and president of the game.

Behind there was the sparkling water; to the right the fertile fields, filled with loaded vineyards; to the left, the distant turrets of a great city, and overhead, the fairest sky that ever canopied a land.

There were successive terraces around the house. Spreading widely out were gardens of paradisaical appearance. Fountains of exquisite design played in every proper place, the bottoms of whose basins were made to reflect the water, and magnify it to startling depths.

Natural beauty, adorned by every suggestion of art, conspired to make this spot beautiful indeed. There were aviaries which excited the wonder of the learned naturalist. Miniature museums were fitted with curious and beautiful specimens; flowers, whose types were not elsewhere known, flourished; the foliage of the spice-trees made the air redolent of perfume. There were artificial fans operated, and a dew created by an expensive apparatus, which, let the day and season be as sultry as they might, made the atmosphere cool and balmy.

Clear streams were turned, and made to run their
course over wires, which caught the liquid woof and
wove it into music.

For fourteen years Electa occupied this beautiful
spot, before we introduce her. Five sons had been
born to her, each one healthy, intelligent, and amiable. In those days gymnastic exercises made an
important branch in young men's education, and
through the exercise of athletic sports our Electa's
sons had strengthened their sinews and secured
elasticity of muscle.

Electa's husband was a Greek, of elegant accom-
plishments. He had been reared among nobles
who were his peers. He was gifted with many virtues; his fine person, set off by graceful manners,
made him a meet companion, in external beauty, for
Electa; while his truly amiable, independent, and
noble spirit created the true congeniality without
which, in wedlock, there can be no true happiness.
He had, whilst a youth, won many prizes for victories achieved in the different branches of art
peculiar to the age and nation.

They had been brought up in the midst of hea-

thendom, where the worship of the living God
Almighty was not known or recognized.

Feasts and observances were held, in which out-
lays were required, of such costliness, brilliance, and
display, as would, if described for our readers,
induce them to imagine that we copied the Genii
of Aladdin's lamp. Games, exercises, and exploits
in wrestling were introduced as a part of the grand
season of Feasts, and Adrian was expert in all.

Electa had met him at the coronal of one of
these matches, where a single wreath of wild olive
was his sole reward for victories which men would
have set any time, labor, and means to accomplish.
Honor was his incentive; no mean impulse ever
actuated him. As Electa was a virgin princess,
she was entitled to an honorable seat on occasion
of feasts.

She first saw Adrian when the highest honor was
conferred upon him that young men ever aspired
to; that of having the year dated with his name;
placed in the calendar, and in front of all laws made
in the same year with the victory. That his name
was thus honored, she herself beheld. He had

carried his ambition of making a great figure in
games as far as any man; and distinguished himself
in the most splendid manner.

In some instances, where Olympic games were
celebrated, ladies were admitted to dispute the prizes.
There are statuary and paintings descriptive of female
victors yet to be seen in ancient cities, but our Electa
was too retiring in her sweet nature to compete with
men for a prize; she was satisfied that her Adrian
should wear all badges of public distinction, and was
contented to shine in the reflected light of his honor.

She married him when he and she both were
worshippers of gods, and amidst the oriental customs, under a tropical sun, lived with him six sweet
years.   But after the death of her grandfather, who
was an Israelite of the tribe of Judah, they removed
to Judea to enjoy their ancestral inheritance.

Old ties called loudly to Adrian to return to his
native land, but the wife and one little boy were so
delighted to remain, that he became persuaded to
content himself, and made his adopted home and
country as dear to his affections as he could.

He often took Electa and her older boys to

Rome, and by narrating the history of pictures, architecture, statues, and scenes to his intelligent children, making every narrative agreeable by traditional description, he hoped to foster a classical taste in their impressible minds, in which wish, from the subsequent history of one, at least, of his sons, he was not disappointed.

Electa, whose beautiful tastes were nurtured to the utmost capability, revelled in all the accessories that a new field of study presented, and she and her husband were wont to visit the ruins of Sodom, the sepulchral shades of the tombs of Absalom and the prophets, and the catacombs; with the law of Moses and the chronicles of the Jews she was so delighted, that every traditionary foot of soil awakened to her reaching mind a new vista through which she beheld the One Great God.

The religion of her forefathers came back to the grandchild as an inheritance; she had cast from her the last vestige of idolatrous opinion, and was to be found in the Tabernacle worshipping with the Israelites, where she first heard of the Jesus of whom the apostles preached.

She was ripe for the New Testament, for she comprehended in the Old the dispensation that should ensue.

In her conformation, elements which constitute the basis for grand action existed, and yet she possessed eminently germs of all the finest, most sensitive susceptibilities of modesty and retirement. She combined the two best qualities of woman—practicability and silence. She was of a disposition more pensile to dictation than *Martha's*, yet somewhat like in activity.

Though, at the time that we introduce her to our readers, of the age of forty, she was not nearly recognizable as that. So fresh and radiant were her personal charms, in fact, that Adrian was furnished with a new remark for each successive birthday anniversary, upon her improved bloom and beauty.

Her skin was of pearly whiteness, with a soft, warm glow of peach in her cheeks : eyes deep blue, tender, and full of love; eyes which talk as well as see. A deep dimple in her chin, which Adrian called the index of her mind; for when the sunshine of smiles came over it, it deepened in sympathy, when seriousness prevailed, it nearly faded out. Her brow was, contrary to the usual contour of Eastern faces, high, of serene and noble character.

Expression was what constituted principally her indescribable loveliness. She was of ordinary height, elastic in her movements, and poetical in her temperamental gestures.

Electa's voice was in itself a charm; through it the slightest emotion was discernible; the most delicate changes of feeling were declared in each inflection. It is, after all, no wonder that she was so lovely, for she was an elect lady, one whom guardian angels sustained, and through whom the holy light was to come, and who was meet to be exalted above an ordinary type.

She was one day relating to her youngest, a bright, blue-eyed boy of six, some oriental fairy tale, when Gaius, her eldest-born, came in, his eyes glistening, his whole face full of excitement; but who was too well-trained, notwithstanding, to give utterance to any impetuous speech.

The mother perceived that something of an interesting and novel nature had occurred, which he was

burning to tell her, who was his confidant and most
intimate companion, but she drew a crimson-colored
velvet cushion nearer to her, merely observing, "Sit
near to mother, my love."

Gaius took off the student's cap from his head,
and let the rich brown curls hang low upon his
neck.

His sensitive nostril dilated, and the red spot
in his cheek indicated unusual excitement, but still
he kept silent, waiting for his mother's invitation to
speak.

The mother's feeling was too tender to allow the
effort for silence longer to pain him, so, after kissing
the little one on her knee, and advising him to go
gently down the flight of steps to the garden, she
turned her face toward Gaius, placed her hand in
his, and with the love-notes of her voice set to
their sweetest cadence, she asked, "What is it, my
son?"

Then the eloquent speech came fast and ardent.
"Mother, I have heard that there is a man called
Jesus who is performing miracles such as none
other, living or dead, has ever done; there is a

rumor that he has brought to life a young girl who
was dead; there are diversities of opinion in regard
to his origin and wonderful power; some contending
that he is of Diabolus, others that he is of the Lord
God, and, Mother, think what a monstrous suggestion! that he is the Lord God himself."

His voice fell to a whisper, his excitement grew
intense. Electa's dimple was gone, the shade of
deep thought was upon her.

For one moment she sent her thoughts tele-
graphing through Jewish tradition; her inspirational monitors crowded her mind and whispered:
"The Messiah!" She believed, she realized, she
rejoiced, and she prophesied.

Never had Gaius heard such words uttered as fell
from the inspired lips of his mother; there seemed
to have come a tongue of fire to point her language,
and under the influence Gaius also became controlled, and they declared together that this Jesus
was the Messiah that sweet-lipped Isaiah had sung
about.

That the revelation of a new dispensation was
inaugurated, and that upon the Old Testament was

to be laid a page which would reveal its mystical pictures, and suit other coming eras.

From this time forth she and Gaius talked together of the prophecies of the old Bible, forming conclusions favorable to their peculiar views.

A beautiful contrast the son and mother afforded, their heads bent together over the same volume, Gaius often raising his face, which was browned by his frequent excursions through the sunshine to Jerusalem; Electa's face by his looking like a drift of snow.

Enthusiastic and devoted, they enjoyed their opinions, and though Adrian was not convinced of the truth of Christ's divine nature, he willingly listened. Adrian was slower to realize the divine light, and not until after Christ's crucifixion and resurrection was he fully converted.

Let our readers imagine after this with what interest Electa watched the course of events concerning the "Son of Man," how every rumor of a new miracle exalted her spirits, how news of his persecution, misappreciation, insult, and neglect, must have pained her, how useless seemed to her

rank, position, wealth, and friends, since he whom
she so sincerely admired, loved, and reverenced, was
an outcast, a wanderer, without a roof to shelter him.

Many plans did her fertile fancy conceive for his
benefit, but of little avail; and never once did she
behold him.

It was after the terrible tragedy of Gethsemane,
when the disciples had been appointed by the risen
Lord to preach; after he ascended to the Father,
and sent his Spirit back to the apostles, which sat
upon them and controlled them to utterances of his
law and will, that Electa began to be most prac-
tically serviceable in the cause of the disciples'
doctrine.

Gaius made personal acquaintance with Jesus,
and was an enthusiastic admirer of the beautiful
Nazarene; he treasured up his sayings to repeat to
his mother, and whenever he could, without giving
offence, he had conveyed to Mary, the mother, who
lived in Bethlehem, gifts of value through Martha
and Mary of Bethany.

After the miraculous resuscitation of Lazarus, the
house of these sisters, and their names, became

traditional among many people far and near, and afterward, when Martha distinguished herself by her beautiful deportment at the feast given to Jesus during the Passover, she especially was much thought of by both friends of Jesus and those opposed to him; for brave and beautiful actions will be recognized by all.

Electa secured every report of the sayings and doings of Jesus, which, from such authority as that of Gaius, she could accredit, and these written manuscripts were afterward very valuable in the compilation of the Gospels.

Many of Electa's proud friends regarded her slightingly, and sneered at her "foolish superstition."

Some even went so far as to declare that she was insane, and others discarded her from their entertainments, slighted her by indignities of non-recognition when they met in public, and in many ways besides they evinced contempt.

Electa was human, therefore was not impervious to slights; her tender feelings were often grievously hurt at the disaffection of those in whom she had reposed confidence, and regarded as friends

She made every advance that dignity would allow, but finally ceased to endeavor to conciliate those whom she knew had no real grounds for their offensive conduct.

She remained apart from them as their conduct suggested,·and in the heart of her family found repose.

She received inward grace and instruction, which was worth more than all the assurances from those friends who in other days had expressed so much, yet who, upon a trivial turn of mere sentiment, had proved themselves, though mighty in pomp and power, hollow in heart, false in affection, and failing in friendship.

In these days of her isolation from the society of the gay world, she formed acquaintance with some of the disciples, and was richly compensated for the loss of some who had professed the strongest interest in her, by the pleasant and instructive visits they made to her house.

The mother of Jesus was a person of uncommon interest to Electa, and when she was informed of her anxiety and great grief, at the perils to which her beloved son was exposed, Electa, with all the woman's tenderness and the mother's sympathy stirring in her bosom, indited a letter to the anxious mother, in which there was the outpouring of genuine sympathy and sincerity, which rejoiced the heart of Mary.

Electa invited her to make a visit to her house, hoping thereby to be able to minister somewhat to her comfort; but Mary was a careful mother, a busy housekeeper, in moderate circumstances, and had no time to make visits.

Gaius increased in learning as well as stature, and was head of his classes in the colleges. His father designed him for the law, but this Gaius believed unsuited to his talents.

His mother's heart dwelt with honest pride upon her first-born, and in the twilight of evening might often be seen the two in confidential conference; the son, understanding the sorrow of the mother for the troubles of Jesus, strove to mitigate her grief by pointing to the high hope which might be presumed Jesus entertained, of being delivered from his enemies and established upon a throne; but

Electa's spiritual vision extended beyond the material plane, and she realized that Christ's kingdom
was not of changing, earthly character, but of an
immortal, eternal foundation in the future world.

Adrian listened to Electa and Gaius, who dis-
cussed their faith in the infallibility of Jesus, and
of his being really the Messiah, as one who is
anxious to believe, and who is yet held back by
some unfortunate vein of constitutional skepticism,
and he sometimes ventured to remonstrate with his
Electa upon the danger of becoming too much
absorbed in a belief for which there was no settled
basis.

"Sweet wife," he would say, "I love you too well
not to be happy to see you enjoy whatever con-
vinces your judgment and accords with your intentions, but possibly this man may not be aught more
than other men.

"For his character I have great esteem; but I
hear it said that he takes no great honor to himself,
and that he openly declares he can, of himself, do
nothing, save what the Father gives him.

"Were he what some infatuated zealots describe,

would he be despised, poor, and lowly as he is? Would he not assert his supremacy by triumphing over his enemies?"

Electa would, at such points, lay her hand over his mouth and beg him to desist.

Adrian listened to her exposition of the theory, but Electa's prophetic teaching was not to be comprehended by his matter-of-fact mind.

He judged as men judge, and not by the spirit, yet he sought to know more; and when the news of the accusation and trial of Jesus met his ears, he went to Jerusalem, was present at the trial, heard the decision, and was one who joined in bringing a plea for the innocent man, against whom no charge could be laid other than that of healing the sick, bringing the dead to life, restoring the sight of the blind, and curing lunatics.

But of no avail was his plea; the decree went forward into effect. Barrabas was released and Jesus was offered up upon the cross.

After the terrible tragedy, dreading the effect that this sad news would have upon his beloved wife,

Adrian, upon his return from Jerusalem, was careful to approach the subject warily.

When Electa saw him coming, she took hold of the hand of the household pet, their youngest-born, and, with the alacrity of a girl, ran down the broad flight of steps which led from the terrace, and out into the avenue.

Adrian beheld her, sprang from his chariot, went forward, and in a moment had her in his arms. There was a silent expression in the nervous touch of his hand, the peculiar earnestness of his embrace, which conveyed to the quick senses of the wife that something unusual was stirring in the soul of him who was her double self; but with her usual refinement of prudence she kept silence, only pressed her face more closely to his bosom, and once more caressed his lips.

Little Marcellus, clamorous for his share of attention, made good excuse for Adrian to hide his emotion, and taking in his arms the intelligent, beautiful little fellow, he started forward with the words, " Come, my precious," to Electa.

After Marcellus had lavished a score of infantile

endearments upon his father, a thought seemed to
control his sympathetic mind; he glanced at his
mother, then at his father, and said: "Father, tell
my mother about Jesus of Nazareth." Electa's eyes
flew to Adrian's; alas! she read disaster and tribu-
lation for the Christ in Adrian's look.

Unable to keep silence longer, she exclaimed:
"Tell me, Adrian, what has happened. I feel, I
know, that some calamity has overtaken that holy
man."

Adrian drew her with his left arm to his side,
glad to escape the inquisition of her eyes, and slowly
answered, "My wife, there has indeed happened to
the Nazarene a great tragedy, an awful fate; but as
you have faith in his immortality, and in the divinity
of his nature, you should not tremble when I relate
that he is already, according to your doctrine, with
'The Father.' As a soldier of his cross, you must
not flinch when I tell you that 'The Son of Man'
was executed yesterday upon a cross.

"Think of him only as your Lord, who is beyond
the need of your tears. To his mother and those
excellent women who must be plunged into irreme-

10

diable grief turn your thoughts, call up your practical talents, and let your generosity, free and un-
conditional as it always is, extend toward them;
strive to comfort them by acts of attention, command me, command our means, give full play to
your principles of benevolence in this terrible crisis.

My heart bleeds for *them*, my wife, not for him,
whose countenance bore the impress of peace and
power. Never, never, have I seen face of man shine
as did the face of Jesus." ·

Electa was fainting; hastily putting the little boy
from his arms, he took her in his tender hold, went
to one of the nearest fountains, laid her sweet form
upon the green grass, dipped up water and held it
to her lips, calling her by every endearing appella-
tion which his aroused anxieties suggested.

These tender love remedies restored her. She
sat up, but shed no tears, only repeated the words:
" Ascended to the Father."

As she gradually realized the sad fact of the suffering of the beloved Christ, she was overwhelmed
with tears, which had the effect of relieving her.

She seated herself in a bower, and with her head

buried in Adrian's bosom, listened to the whole story which he graphically related.

When he concluded, she raised her eyes to heaven, clasped her hands, and vowed that so long as she might live she would never again repine, let come whatever affliction there might.

I will emulate this patient Lord, who, though the floodgates of trial were opened upon him, never shrank from a cheerful performance of duty, never gave vent to complaint, and was never heard to murmur.

By the time that Gaius, who was in Rome, returned, the common wonder and interest of the people was stirred into thrilling inquiry of the probability of the Divine nature of the martyr. The forms which came up from the graves and walked openly before the people, the darkness that had settled over the world, the obscurity of the sun, the earthquake, were all supernatural phenomena, and his words, parables, and sayings, became familiarly quoted by all classes.

No man who had ever lived became so famous after death.

Electa's health suffered somewhat, and about a year after this, her husband, who was watchful of the least varying shade in her condition, solicitous to the most lover-like anxiety, prevailed on her to go with him to Athens, where she might secure the best medical advice.

After Electa had selected many articles of utility, and dispatched them to Mary, the mother of Jesus, who was very poor, with a large family to superintend, and many domestic cares besides the burden of her son's death, she and her two youngest children, their attendant, and Adrian, went to the renowned city of Athens.

Electa recovered her bloom and usual elasticity, and sought the most intricate portions of the town, in search of historic places and scenery.

One day, as she passed a house on the outskirts of the suburbs, she heard voices singing sweet hymns of a spiritual character; there was something so wondrously plaintive in the nature of the strains that she begged Adrian to go with her to the very spot, to ascertain who were the singers. Adrian, who refused her nothing, accorded his compliance, and, after winding up several pairs of stairs, they found themselves in a large room, in which was assembled a large number of men and women.

Electa had never seen any form of worship besides the heathen worship, and that of the Jewish tabernacle. Her own heart knew its own forms, but the rites, postures, and the peculiar usages of the disciples she had never witnessed.

The song ended, here was one man kneeling with hands clasped and eyes raised, while his voice ascended in the most earnest supplication to an invisible power; all the rest of the assembly were also kneeling, with their heads bent in their open palms; to the risen Christ the appeal was made. It was a little band of men persecuted and afraid, who had been baptized with inspiration, and were *en rapport* with the ascended Jesus; a company of disciples of whom she had heard, but never before had met.

Her heart burned within her; she stood contemplating the scene until the prayer was ended; then, being observed by the meeting, seats were offered to Adrian and herself, and they also rested.

Silas and Timotheus conducted this little meeting; each spoke with burning eloquence of their knowledge of the soul's immortality; they related their experiences of seeing and conversing with Jesus after his resurrection, and cited the instance of John's witnessing the transfiguration on the Mount, when the spirits of Moses and Elias had manifested themselves.

Imagine the enthusiasm of our beautiful Electa as she drank in these accounts, which so well accorded with her own impressional experience. Adrian was *there* converted to a full belief in the doctrines of the apostles, and much cause had Electa to rejoice that she had followed the sound of the sacred singing on that ever well-remembered evening.

Frequently after this Electa went with Adrian to the meetings of the disciples, and her ready zeal gave an impetus to many who were nearly lost in doubt.

The things that the apostles did were of so startling a nature that many hesitated between two beliefs, some imputing their gifts to an evil source.

At Athens, Electa took her little boys to the feasts of idolatry, which were celebrated with great splendor; she wished them to be informed on every point, to be able to form opinions and to judge all subjects for themselves.

Athens at that time was almost wholly given to idolatry.

Philosophers of the Epicureans and Stoics had great influence, and when the moral teaching of the disciples, which prescribed temperance and moderation, reached, through report, their ears, they were greatly offended, and thought that it was an effort to introduce new gods; and yet the Athenians were a wonder-loving people, were continually searching for novelty, and when some of them heard of Jesus, they erected a sign which bore the inscription, "TO THE UNKNOWN GOD," and blindly and ignorantly worshipped this "god" because of *the novelty*. There were others who were afraid of the power, and sought to confute the ablest advocates of Jesus.

In this new and exciting field, Electa's fine mind was exercised to study, and she embraced very rapidly the most advanced thoughts.

She visited all places, and made good use of the opportunity to store the young intellects of her boys with information which, in the future, would be valuable.

In maturer years these boys realized the benefit of having had so intelligent a mother to control their infantile minds, and secure them the education which her peculiarly sound judgment had made her conscious would be profitable and advantageous.

Upon Mars' hill often might be seen Adrian and Electa with the little boys, Marcellus and Alexander; to these Adrian pointed out beauties in architecture, explained dates, and described epochs connected with each. Electa's ingenuity devised many a beautiful scheme for their edification and amusement.

It seems that prosperity had crowned all of Electa's days, for no personal want or calamity had ever befallen her or her household.

Munificence poured in its countless comforts and conveniences; good health had, with partiality, invested each of her children; physical beauty was inherited jointly, from both father and mother, by each son.

It was difficult to determine which boy might ripen into the greatest perfection, so full was each one of promise.

Their princely home bloomed newly, as another year added fuller foliage to the trees, more numerous blossoms, and increase in every fruitful department; flocks were added, ingenious devices which had been brought in vogue were applied, and refinement of art adapted through every avenue to each department.

Nothing failed Adrian; his business capabilities extended to the minutest detail of finance, and revenue seemed to flow naturally to his demand.

Through these years of ceaseless prosperity, Electa had been universally charitable.

She practised benevolence and exercised charity continuously; was never arrogant, but, with sweet humility, occupied any place, however obscure, in which her presence and means might effect comfort and blessing.   Tried by no sudden and absolute

10*

reverse, the true metal of her nature had not as yet been tested.

As a pampered child of fortune, we have so far known Electa.

It was in the spring-time, after Electa had been in Athens a year, when Adrian thought it best to return home and leave Gaius to make a tour of the Nile with his mother.

Electa's heart was pained at the separation, and, as she twined her arms about her beloved Adrian, forebodings of tragic, possible accident occurred to her. "I feel, I realize, Adrian," she said, "that terror and catastrophe are rising in our sky; heretofore we have had no adverse winds, now a tempest is brewing; something tells me so, and yet I do not know what voice it is that whispers to me; my Adrian, my best beloved, remember, let happen what will, that our hearts are one, our minds are one." Adrian kissed away her tears, soothed her fears, and, by gentle persuasion, prepared her for the moment of parting.

"You, my birdie," he said, "have not yet learned to fly without me. Silence your apprehensions, enjoy your trip, and return to me with blooming color, and in robust health. Nothing that I have seen in Athens can half-way compare with the beauty of my Electa's eyes."

Theatres were the resort of all who aspired to high art, and histrionic representation was then the best school for literary students.

Philosophers and sages hung suspended upon the mimic utterances of the drama, and stored their minds with hints of modes for future reformation of vice through this powerful avenue.

After Adrian left, Electa went with Gaius to the great theatre, to see a performance which was in high vogue. It was there that Gaius for the first time beheld Persis; loved her upon first sight, and to whom he was afterward happily united in wedlock.

It happened that the two families were at the same time tourists, and upon the banks of the most renowned river in the world, amidst the romance and blush of beautiful scenery, peace-engendering atmospheres, and harmonious circumstances, youth took on its sweetest, holiest, strongest, and freshest attitude, and discovered love.

The hearts of Persis and Gaius were like the mellow June morning, which emits the odors that the earth and air and sun and cloud have made the most redolent in sweets, and which by its own ardor fixes in one great realization.

Their impressible affections received the touches of the inspirer, adapted every pleasing, passing strain to help make full the diapason of melody, harmony, and time. Their courtship moved on oiled hinges, for there were no disapproving guardians to interfere.

Persis was a Jewess, liberal in thought, and much affected by the teaching of Paul, who had for a short time preached in Athens; when the whole city seeming bent upon idolatry, he had, in the very teeth of danger, ventured to present Christ's doctrine. She was afterward converted, and fully entered into all plans of Gaius and Electa, for the support of the elders and scattered brethren.

This was a season of especial pleasure to Electa; her forebodings wore off, she encouraged joy, and took hold of amusement with all the ardor of her enthusiastic nature.

When the sunset gilded the landscape, when the moon alone trod the sky, when their heavy vessel dipped deep and ploughed through the surge, she was impressible either to the sublime or appreciative of the romantic.

Marcellus kept a cabinet filled with each days' spoils, and Alexander saved specimens of plants and shells, which his mother took great pains to arrange.

Women were regarded in high esteem in a day and age when some of the most powerful monarchs that ever sat upon a throne were of that sex.

Among the Jews also women served in the tabernacle and were prophetesses, whose oracles were sought after and adopted by philosophers and sages.

Woman was not oppressed and secondarily regarded, by any means, but they were responsible money-holders, merchants, and preachers.

Women spoke in public and exhorted in private assemblies. St. Paul, the celebrated orator, like all great geniuses, had peculiarities of opinion; woman was to him evidently a sealed book; he disapproved of the custom of the women of the period to exhort and speak, and advised them against it.

Some of the Hebrew women were especially earnest, strong, and deep in character; of clear, comprehensive intellects; ardent and devout in temperament. They were unlike the listless, supine orientals generally, and though domestic and meek, being contented in the sphere of home, they sometimes made a wider sphere or went beyond, as their talents directed.

Deborah had long before prophesied, been inspired, and recited inspirational poems which were full of burning beauty and melting pathos. She also went out and sat under the shade of the palm-trees, and fearlessly judged Israel.

Her name was famous among men, reverenced by the tribes, and handed down to posterity in connection with some of the most startling prose poems that ever medium uttered; she was full of the inspiration of genius, and was not afraid to speak it publicly. She even took part in the battles.

The quiet incidents of Electa's record were written chiefly through the hearts of her home circle. She had governed her household actively and diligently, and had been well reported of by her neighbors and strangers. She had relieved the afflicted, and had poured oil into many a wounded spirit; had diligently followed every good work.

She was a holy mother, a noble woman, who was fit and meet to be a follower of Christ. To perpetuate his principles and practise his divine example was her desire, in which she most happily succeeded. To her husband she had been the guiding star of life, the beacon of his aspiration, and the anchor of his hopes.

"Woman! blest partner of our joys and woes;
　Even in the darkest hour of earthly ill,
Untarnished yet thy fond affection glows,
　Throbs with each pulse, and beats with every thrill
When sorrow rends the heart, when feverish pain
　Wrings the hot drops of anguish from the brow,—
To soothe the soul, to cool the burning brain,
　Oh! who so welcome and so prompt as thou?"

This was what Electa was to Adrian. But through rosy paths her life had always led, and no great trial of her virtues or sacrifice of ease had ever been called for. The time was near which

would unfold the lofty attributes, the unflinching
bravery of our Electa.

After a most charming season had lent its bland-
ishments to heap up pleasure to our travellers, when
the spring and summer were over, and Gaius and
his beloved Persis had settled all preliminaries, and
were only waiting for a convenient day to solemnize
their nuptials, a letter came to Electa full of apprehensions of a terrible persecution which threatened
the Christians.

Rumors had reached Adrian of the confiscation
of property, of fire and sword, and in one or
two instances, of the murders of several Christians. Electa knew Adrian's habit of thought
too well to suppose that any rumor of a trivial
character or uncertain foundation would be sufficient to induce him to impart news which might
possibly alarm her.

She hastily made preparation for instant return,
and, in company with the young bride and groom,
she reached home just as the yellow began to
paint the foliage, and fruit was golden with ripeness.

Tender was the meeting of husband and wife-
and of mother and boys, who had been brought
from school to meet her, but mixed with melancholy and mystery, for Adrian was evidently concealing a secret; in every tone of his voice apprehension was discernible.

The lovely spot was lovelier than ever; nothing
was neglected; beauty sat on everything.

Marcellus and Alexander were wild with exuber-
ance of delight at meeting their father and brothers,
and Gaius, too happy in his new relation of husband, went hither and thither with his bride,
revealing each day some unobserved corner in
which a rare bird had its nest, a fountain sent its
waters through mystical jets, or some attraction of
delightful import met the senses.

Meanwhile, a week passed, and amidst the de-
lights of reunion, the general bustle of getting
settled, Electa had not looked as deeply into
Adrian's mind, or weighed his peculiarity of manner as she would have done under ordinary, quiet
circumstances; but at the end of that time, as she,
Gaius, and Persis were occupied in some trivial
individual concerns, a traveller arrived.

To Gaius, the appearance of John the Evangel-
ist was indescribably pleasing. There had, for a
long time, been an intimacy between these two
young Christians, and John was most tenderly attached to Electa. He had often been heard to say
that every Christian, every female virtue, centred in
this chosen one.

Sorrowful was his face on this occasion, when
Electa, after having kissed him, proceeded, with
her own fair hands, according to the custom among
Jews and Christians, to wash his feet.

Alas, he had nothing but recitals of trial and
trouble and persecution to relate.

The Christians were pursued, hunted out, and
beaten down; no one who acknowledged the
religion of the cross was safe from the penalty of
the severest cruelties.

He told her of horrible scenes, and to Adrian,
and Gaius, and Persis as well, related the events
which had lately transpired under his own notice.

He himself had been subjected to the greatest
straits; he dared not follow his peculiar business,
his very tools were subject to the most unreason-

able fines, and nobody would give their countenance to a disciple for fear of punishment in one form or another.

Electa's tears flowed abundantly, her sympathetic heart burned within her, and she longed to be able to manifest her devotion by practical work.

After John left them, much comforted and refreshed, Electa's house became a refuge and a hospital for the persecuted, foot-sore, weary Christians; weary only in limb, not in spirit.

Nothing could exceed the tenacity with which they unflinchingly clung to the faith of Jesus. Persis, with her own fair hands made useful articles of clothing, nursed the sick, bound up wounds, and performed menial offices for pilgrim Christians.

Everything that their vast wealth had for years been storing came willingly into the hands of its owners for the use of these afflicted ones.

It began to get unsafe for Adrian or Gaius to appear in public; rumors had reached the rulers of their proclivities, and, although their high position and vast wealth gave them wide privilege, and consequence of no mean extent, they were yet not safe from the prejudices under which religious zeal, the most violent of all incentives, laid them.

Gaius noticed the lowering brow, the suppressed murmurs, when his presence at any public meeting was noticed, and although his loyalty would have borne any test, yet his prudence pointed to him that it was best for him not to hasten any catastrophe.

Electa realized inwardly, through her perceptive powers, that there was a heavy calamity impending.

Active benevolent enterprise, in behalf of positive sufferers, sufficed to keep up her spirits; for her husband, her children, she dreaded the fate that she saw fixed.

For herself, her faith was sufficient to convince her of her future immortality; she was not glad to leave the scene of life, but of her fate, as she said, she was fully convinced.

Flocks and herds, money and provender, were all at the disposal of refugees and mourners. Much suffering there was now, and to her general sorrow there came a heart-rending, personal, family affliction.

During twenty-eight years of married life they

had never lost a child. At this season their intelligent, promising second son, David, died, and was buried in the great ancestral tomb which had for thirty years been unvisited by a new tenant.

To all mothers who know this heart-rending grief our Electa will be an object of sympathy. She could not be rebellious to the will of God, but, as a mother, the strings of her heart were painfully strained.

Afflictions came thick and heavy after this.

From a disease of the optical nerve, Adrian became blind, first in one eye, then in both. It was a piteous sight to behold this model of manly beauty stricken down with darkness; to know that through the rest of his days no light of sun, moon, or stars was to gild his pathway : that through his Electa any avenue could alone be trod; only through her was life to be kept worth the having.

And Electa ? In the last year her beautiful hair had grown gray, lines of care began to seam her brow and crease her cheek, and the rich color which had been remarkable in her complexion was waning into pallor; but with the depreciation of her physical bloom there was a more *holy* beauty shed over her countenance, the perfect reflection of the spiritual growth within.

Their revenue was still large, but owing to the enormous taxation and other unusual drains, Gaius, who had now the control of his father's business, found it necessary to retrench and economize.

These beautiful grounds and fine mansion were the common resort for the afflicted Christians scattered throughout the country, and Electa's name was a talisman to many a fainting heart. St. John hesitated not to claim her clemency, but made use of her liberality in all cases of distress that came immediately under his notice.

Adrian sat about the garden with Electa or Marcellus by his side nearly the half of every day. He was inclined to melancholy, which added to Electa's distress. His beautiful resignation to the affliction which had befallen him proved his submission and firm reliance upon a high Power, but his human nature would *sometimes* lament.

After the family had been returned from the Nile

for about one year, Persis gave birth to a lovely babe, a little girl. Gaius was exceedingly proud of his little treasure, and more devoted than ever to its mother.

When this little bud was four months old, Persis one day took it to a seat, near to the farthest fountain, which was occupied by Adrian. She laid it in his lap. Adrian caressed its little hands and feet, while *the baby* was delighted to twist its little fingers in the beard of Adrian, which crept like a drift of snow and lay upon the baby's form.

While the young mother knelt upon the sward watching with indescribable delight the intelligent glance of her first-born's dark-brown eyes, several men approached.

Persis' heart beat. She knew that something unusual was astir, for these men were officers in the king's uniform.

Hastily clasping her babe in her arms, her next thought was for Electa, and she flew back through the nearest avenue, and found Electa busy with the services of the supper-hour, for she always superintended, and with her own hands helped to arrange,

supper: "Mother! mother!" cried Persis, "there
are soldiers in the garden talking to father."

Electa gave one swift, startled look toward her
daughter-in-law, then calming herself, silently and
majestically awaited what she felt would be a catastrophe.

Soon the same men, whom Electa's quick eyes
had perceived were armed with high authority,
came confidently up the steps and forward into the
pavilion, where Electa still stood rooted to the spot;
but when they came near enough to perceive the
beauty of her countenance, and its expression of
strength and determination, they altered involuntarily their manner, and stood at first with bowed
heads, respectfully awaiting her speech. "Where-
fore, friends, are ye come?" inquired she, calmly.

Then one, stepping forward, produced a scroll of
parchment, and from it read the decree of the king.
To this effect it ran, that all who confessed the
doctrine of Christ were commanded to recant, or to
be punished with imprisonment, trial, and perhaps
death.

The foremost speaker then took from under

his cloak a wooden cross, and placing it upon the floor, explained to Electa that, by simply placing her foot upon it, he would understand that she resigned her peculiar faith, and that she would be secure from any indignity or penalty.

In an instant the dream that, many years ago, as related in the opening of our narrative, had disturbed her, flashed before her mental vision, and she realized its fulfillment.

She stood unflinchingly before the officer, who, touched by her chaste beauty and evident superiority, endeavored to persuade her to take the step which would save them, for he plainly told her that each one of her family would alike have to suffer.

Of course, Electa refused; she meekly folded her hands; then, in obedience to the sentence they uttered, she let them be manacled.

Adrian, Gaius, Persis, and the next eldest boys were taken first to Jerusalem, were subsequently transported to Rome, and imprisoned.

There was some consideration shown the females, yet, for all that, the sufferings which they endured were intense. No friendship, no love, was sufficient to save them from the hardship incidental to prison life, and in six months our beautiful women, as well as the stouter men, were invalids, weak and pale, shadows of their former selves, but still buoyant in zeal, and resolved, if need be, to suffer martyrdom rather than renounce a religion in which they believed.

Adrian and Electa sang hymns sometimes, and the stern jailor many a time wiped tears from his eyes, as, when instead of threats and complaint, he heard them pray for their enemies.

At the expiration of one year the Roman judge offered them another opportunity to recant. They refused, which was a sign of their death-warrant.

Our sympathies are fain to close now, before the drama reaches the final act, tragical and horrible as it was; but our readers who have gone with us so far, would not be satisfied unless we showed them the *finale;* and, painful as is the task, we will yet, for their sakes, paint the scene of their end, in as moderate colors as the vivid subject will allow.

The whole world of air, heaven, light, and motion,

was in its holiday garb, for it was the season of the
year when nature seems to be decked on purpose
for some gala festival, when Electa, wrapped in a
scarlet gown, was seen behind the jailor, holding in
convulsive clasp the head of her Adrian; again and
again she pressed his sightless eyes to her bosom;
then taking leave of her Gaius, her eldest-born, and
Persis, her fond and faithful daughter-in-law, and
successively of her children and grandchild, she
told the jailor good-bye, and thanked him for his
kindness to her and hers, was then rudely led forward by men of herculean forms, who fastened her
to the heels of oxen, which were driven around the
public squares.

She was not suffered to expire in this way, but
with the extreme refinement of cruelty, they restored
her exhausted faculties by administering stimulants,
and then, in the face of a large multitude, fastened
her to a cross, where she, with these words on her
lips, "Father, forgive them, they know not what
they do," expired.

The sun had not sent its last rays of gold over the
scene ere Adrian, Gaius, and all the others, save

Marcellus and Alexander, were victims to the same barbarism.

Owing to the tender ages of Marcellus and Alexander they were spared, though their patrimony was not allowed them.

They devoted themselves to the infant left by Persis, and the educations which they had received secured them means of employment in schools of juvenile students; afterward they were professors in the university; and, after the furor subsided, and men grew more tolerant of the Christian religion, they became distinguished as teachers and preachers; but the tragedy of that golden sunset never laid its shadow. It was a memory which haunted them through all their subsequent lives.

www.ingramcontent.com/pod-product-compliance
Lightning Source LLC
Chambersburg PA
CBHW030811020726
47499CB00006B/1873